McALLISTER MAKES WAR

Vengeance was what McAllister wanted
. . . Vengeance for his friend, shot
down right in front of his eyes.
Vengeance against the toughest, cruel-
lest, all-fired meanest operator the West
had ever seen, a man who took what he
wanted just whenever he wanted it.
Rem McAllister set out to avenge his
friend and clean up the town.

MATT CHISHOLM

McALLISTER MAKES WAR

Complete and Unabridged

LINFORD
Leicester

First published in Great Britain in 1969 by
Panther Books Ltd,
London

First Linford Edition
published December 1986

British Library CIP Data

Chisholm, Matt
  McAllister makes war.—Large print ed.—
Linford western library
Rn: Peter Watts   I. Title
823′.914[F]   PR6073.A8/

ISBN 0-7089-6289-0

Published by
F. A. Thorpe (Publishing) Ltd.
Anstey, Leicestershire
Set by Rowland Phototypesetting Ltd.
Bury St. Edmunds, Suffolk
Printed and bound in Great Britain by
T. J. Press (Padstow) Ltd., Padstow, Cornwall

1

McALLISTER was twenty-three years old, he was six foot one inch in his sox, broad in the shoulder and slim in the hip. He was fancy-free, he was broke and he didn't give a damn. The gun he wore at his hip was an old cap-and-ball Remington converted to cartridge and had been given to him by his father some ten years before. It had a scarred cedar butt that was worn smooth by much handling.

He walked down the main street of Combville, Kansas, and looked for the likeliest saloon. The Longhorns caught his eye and appealed to him as a Texan. He'd know some of the boys in there. He went through the batwing doors like a small tornado and surveyed the scene— smoke and the smell of drink was heavy on the still air, the place was crowded and full of the noise of conversation. Some drank, some played cards, some did br *h. The bar ran the whole length of the and was crowded. McAllister ran his along it until it stopped at a tall man with Irish railroader written all over him.

McAllister gave a pleased grunt, elbowed his way through the crowd until he stood behind the tall man. He tapped him on the shoulder, the Irishman turned, frowning. McAllister pulled him away from the bar and hit him. It was what might be called a playful blow with no real intent to do damage behind it. But it staggered the Irishman a dozen feet backward, sent him into a table and landed him with the table on its side on the floor. The card players who occupied it jumped to their feet with startled and indignant cries.

The Irishman picked himself up, he looked surprised and offended.

"What did you do that for?" he asked mildly.

"Because I feel good," McAllister told him.

The Irishman wiped his nose with the

back of his hand, walked slowly up to McAllister and hit him full in the face with a fist that looked as if it could fell a Kentucky mule. It lifted the big man from his feet and sent him into the awed spectators. Willing hands hurled him back into the arena and toward the waiting fists of the Irishman who hit him again, this time in the belly. McAllister doubled up and the Irishman hit him under the chin and knocked him head over heels back into the crowd. Generously, they returned him. He ran head down straight into the Irishman, caught him in the belly, knocked the wind out of him and put him on his back. The building shook to its foundations.

The Irishman sat up.

"Jesus," he said.

He climbed to his feet.

"By all the indications," he remarked, "you want a fight."

McAllister nodded.

"I got one," he said.

"You can say that again," said the Celtic giant.

A man yelled: "Ten to one on Pat." He was eagerly taken up. The place was bedlam. The barkeep reached for a bungstarter and yelled: "Take your fight outside."

Two stalwarts appeared with blackjacks in their hands. One jerked his head toward the street and said: "Out."

The Irishman looked at McAllister.

"Do I fight you or these two bastards?" he enquired courteously.

McAllister said: "You take the one on the left, Pat, I'll look after the other."

The two bouncers advanced with purpose. McAllister and the Irishman went eagerly to meet them. Men yelled at the tops of their voices as fresh bets were taken. One of the bouncers raised his weapon to strike the Irishman over the head, Pat hit him in the belly, seized him around his neck and hurled him bodily at the bar. The bouncer hit the floor and appeared to be weeping. He got slowly to his feet, but he wasn't there long, for Pat hit him behind the ear and laid him on the planks on his face.

McAllister dodged a swinging black-jack, snapped a right into the bouncer's face, crossed a left to the heart, dropped almost to the floor, gripped the man by the ankles and somersaulted him. The bouncer raised his dust and blood flecked face from the floor and said: "My Gawd." He got heavily to his feet and charged. McAllister sidestepped him, tripped him and sent him into the bar which, under this second assault, nearly collapsed. The wood cracked under the impact of the bouncer's head and sounded like a gunshot.

The barkeep brought a sawnoff shotgun into view and said: "Outside."

A man pushed his way through the crowd, an ordinary-looking man in a storesuit and wearing a hard hat and a large black mustache. McAllister knew him. This was Art Malloy, town marshal, a man of some reputation, tough on Texas cowhands who came up the trail to Kansas and raised hell, but fair. He allowed no firearms in town and jailed anybody seen on the streets with one on his hip. He kept the peace under difficult circumstances.

He wasn't particularly tough, he wasn't the fastest ever with a gun, but he had a lot of nerve. Men feared and respected him. He had been the law here for six months and he had the town tamed. He was an old friend of Rem McAllister's. He looked hard at Rem now, eyed Pat the Irishman and gazed without humor at the two bouncers.

"I'm taking you in, McAllister, and you Pat. Walk down to the jail with me," he said.

Pat said: "Sure, Art, it was only fun."

"Looks like it," Art said, shortly. "Let's get going."

They followed him out of the saloon. Without a word to them the marshal led the way across the street, angling through the dust toward his office. He unlocked the door, lit the lamp and opened the cell that filled one end of the building.

"Just get in there and cool off, boys," he said amiably. They walked inside and he slammed the grill door after them. "I

6

never knew there was anybody could take those two bouncers." He chuckled a little. "Did you eat?"

"No," said McAllister.

"No," said Pat.

"I'll have something sent over from the café later," the marshal told them. He went back to his desk and started on some paper work. The two prisoners sat on the cots provided; the Irishman built a smoke and lit up, McAllister filled his pipe and fired it. When they had smoked, they lay on the cots and dozed. An hour passed before a deputy marshal came in and Malloy sent him over to the café to get the prisoners their supper. The deputy grumbled a little and went. When he came back with a loaded tray, the marshal sent him out onto the street again and brought the tray over to the cell. He slid it under the grilled door and said: "On the town, boys. Eat hearty. Can you pay your fine, Rem?"

"Don't have a cent," McAllister told him.

The marshal thought about that.

"How much is it?" Pat asked.

"Five dollars flat charge."

"I'll pay it."

McAllister said: "Thanks."

"Mighty civil of you," said the marshal.

The street door opened and two men walked in. The marshal turned. McAllister yelled: "Look out," for he had seen the bandannas over the lower part of their faces and the levelled shotgun. He flung himself down to the floor, glimpsing Malloy also going down, his right hand pulling the colt gun from its sheath.

The shotgun roared, making a deafening noise in the confined space. The place was full of black smoke. The marshal was hurled back against the bars. The gun roared again. It seemed that pellets flew all around McAllister.

One of the men shouted: "He's dead. Light a shuck."

They turned and ran out onto the street.

McAllister was on his feet, half-stunned by the noise of the shooting.

"Art," he said.

The marshal raised a torn and blood-stained face.

"Help me, Rem," he whispered.

McAllister knelt down, reached through the bars and felt the keys in the man's pocket. He took them out and awkwardly unlocked the door. He and the Irishman stepped out. Now that Pat had a good look at the marshal, he gasped in horror. It seemed that the buckshot had torn open the whole of the man's front. Together, they lifted him and placed him on one of the cots in the cell.

McAllister asked: "Is there a doctor in town?"

"Sure, I'll get him."

The Irishman turned and ran out of the building. McAllister got to work on Malloy. He ripped open his torn and bloody shirt, pulled down the pants' top. The damage the shotgun had done was terrible. He had never seen such an injury in his life before and didn't know where to begin; the whole belly and the chest were lacerated and bleeding. The right

9

arm seemed to have been torn open. He got Malloy's jacket off, removed the marshal's necktie and tied it around the upper arm as a tourniquet. He tore his own bandanna from around his neck and tried to stop the body wounds. It was like trying to stop a flood. He doubted Malloy could live before the doctor got there.

The marshal opened his eyes.

"I'm a goner, Rem."

"We'll fix you up, Art," McAllister told him.

"They made a sieve of me."

"Holiest lawman I ever saw."

A man came in from the street on the run. It was the deputy marshal. He came and looked down at Malloy, aghast.

"You do this?" he demanded of McAllister.

"Yeah," the big man snarled, "that's why I'm still here. You got any clean rag?"

The man said: "A shirt do?"

"Anything, but make it quick."

The man went into a rear room and came back a moment later with a clean white shirt. McAllister tore it up and made pads of it, telling the deputy to help him plug the wounds. Several men came from the street and wanted to know what the shooting was. They came to the door of the cell and gaped at the wounded man, attracted to blood like flies. McAllister roared for them to get the hell out of there. They seemed reluctant to go and wanted to know who he thought he was. With the use of some choice language and the threat of his fists, they went. He returned to Malloy.

"Who did it?" he asked.

Malloy said: "Could have been anybody of a dozen. I have plenty of enemies."

He closed his eyes.

They worked away at the bleeding and finally Pat returned with the doctor, a pale-faced man in a dark suit. He put his bag on the cot, took a look at Malloy, straightened up and said: "I can't do anything here. This man's dead."

The deputy made a strangled noise. McAllister gave him a glance and saw the

11

man was overcome with emotion. The doctor picked up his bag.

"There's nothing I can do," he said again. "This is a bad day for this town. Art Malloy was a good man. He held the lid on this inferno."

A short fat man walked into the office and said: "What in God's name's going on here?"

The doctor said: "Somebody killed Art Malloy."

The fat man looked as if he were going to faint.

"Who's this?" McAllister demanded.

The doctor said: "This is the mayor."

Homer T. Touch. McAllister knew of him—a fancy dresser, a man with interest in the cattlepens in town and a lover of fine horses which he liked to race. He now had a small handkerchief out and was wiping his face.

"Who did it?" he demanded and was told that nobody knew. This was terrible; the killers must be hunted down and brought to justice at once. What would the town do without Malloy? For six months he had kept the peace in a wide-open town. Who could replace him?

"Carson," he said to the deputy, "you must take over meanwhile. You'll never replace Art, but you'll have to do your best. I'll see that you have adequate assistance."

The deputy gulped and looked flustered.

McAllister said: "If the deputy's job's open, I'll take it."

They all turned and stared at him.

"Who is this man?" piped the mayor.

"Name's Remington McAllister," McAllister told him.

"Any relation to Chad McAllister?"

"He was my daddy."

"By God, if you're anything like your old man, you'll do."

After that, they went their various ways; Pat back to the saloon because he reckoned the killing had upset his stomach something terrible; the mayor dashed off to consult the town council; the doctor went back to the game of cards he had left. McAllister and the deputy were left with the corpse.

McAllister said: "You got a drink around here?"

"Sure."

The deputy found a bottle in a desk drawer and poured for the two of them. They drank.

"The name's Jim Carson," said the deputy.

"Glad to know you," McAllister said and they shook.

"How come you volunteered for the job of deputy?"

"Malloy was a friend of mine from way back."

"And he arrested you."

"He'd of jailed his own mother."

McAllister looked at the deputy for the first time. He was several years older than McAllister, fair haired and bearded. He looked like a man who could handle himself, but he didn't look much like a leader.

"What's the pay here?" McAllister demanded.

"You'll get sixty a month."

"It'll keep the wolf from the door."

They had another drink and then Carson said: "Hold the fort, I'll go get the undertaker to take care of Malloy." He went out. McAllister went into the cell and picked up Malloy's gunbelt and gun from the floor.

"I'll kill the son of a bitch that did this with this gun," he said aloud. It wasn't the right attitude for a lawman to take, but he took it just the same.

2

THE next morning when Carson was on his way to his bed and McAllister was ready for the quiet morning stint, McAllister over a cup of coffee in the office asked: "Jim, you have any ideas on who could have killed Malloy?"

"Too many candidates," Carson said.

"Name me some."

"Some were personal, some were official as you might say," was the reply. "There was Fred Darcy he had a run in with only last week." McAllister knew Darcy, a wild Texan, one of two brothers who ran the Golden Fleece on Garrett Street. He would have hated Malloy just because the marshal was a northerner. Darcy was a drink-crazy homicidal maniac with at least six dead men to his credit. "Then there was Fritz Commer of the Longhorns, he tried to buy Malloy

16

off over some petty offense or other and Malloy took him in front of the judge. You know how Malloy was about his personal honesty. Then there was Will Drummond who owns a good deal of this town. But that was personal. There was a lady involved, but I know it nearly came to guns one time. There was all the small fry from down the trail who took a drink too many and threatened to kill Malloy when he took their guns away. Any one of them might have done it. They really hated him. You'll know he fought for the north during the war. They didn't forget that."

"Did he ever kill anybody in town?"

"Just one."

"When was this?"

"First day he put the badge on. We expected trouble from the drovers when he clamped down on the no-gun ordinance straight off. The cowboys all swore they'd get him, but it was mostly hot air. It was funny, really—the real threat came from a Yankee—Wild Jack Little."

McAllister sat up.

"Judas Priest," he exclaimed, "Art didn't brace Little, did he?"

"The other way around. It was a matter of pride with Wild Jack, I reckon. It was his pleasure, treeing marshals. He bit off more'n he could chew with Art. He braced him right out there on Main in front of the whole town with his horse standing by so he could make a run for it after he had killed the marshal. He got off three shots to Malloy's one, but it was Jack who was dead when the smoke blew away. That put Art right out on top. Nobody was ready to buck the man who had killed Wild Jack Little."

"We have a whole lot of men to look at."

"You said it."

"Jack Little had two brothers. All three were pretty close."

After a little more talk, Carson went off to his bed. McAllister sat thinking. He had seen the Little brothers one time down in Fort Worth. A tough mean trio if ever he had seen one. He wondered if either Marve or Frank Little were in town. He hoped they weren't. He didn't fancy facing those two hombres. They were gun artists of the top rank.

He finished his coffee and went for a look at the town.

He didn't think much of it, though it was growing and showed all the signs of being big some day. Right now most of the town was made of green lumber that was already warping, but there was still some adobe and even soddy about. Here and there some enterprising soul had introduced brick. The banker was one of these. The bank stood at an angle of forty-five degrees from the marshal office, away to the left. It looked stark and bare against the shabby spread of the rest of the town. The banker was opening his door even as McAllister stepped onto what was the beginning of a sidewalk in town.

He strolled along Lincoln and found the place stirring. An ox wagon lumbered down the center of the street, the slow animals walking behind their teamster, a bearded giant of a man with his long whip on his shoulder. A horse-drawn wagon with a team of four rattled by, swaying on the rutted street. A horse-backer or two went by, cantering; a buggy rattled past him. The Longhorns was open, for it never closed. The swamper was at work with mop and broom, working his way around the early drinkers or those who had not stopped drinking since the night before.

McAllister turned into Garrett and had a look at the Golden Fleece owned by the Darcy Brothers who had had a run-in with Art Malloy. Already the paint was flaking off the painting of the golden fleece that decorated its false-front. A drooping man stood outside on the side-walk surveying the morning. He was flashily dressed in clawhammer coat and silk vest, but he looked as though he had slept in his clothes. His fine gray pants were tucked into polished knee-high boots. This McAllister knew was Fred Darcy. Known throughout Texas and the west. A hasty passionate man whose appearance belied his character. To look at he could be a Methodist preacher with a sad face. But he was a heller. Somewhere in Texas he had a wife and three children. In Combville he kept a mistress, drank and ate hearty and made money. He always made money. And lost it. Men said he would gamble on where a fly would fall and they were probably right. He had served as a sergeant in the Texas cavalry during the war, had killed a fellow sergeant and somehow got away with it and had deserted before the end of the war. A good many sheriffs wanted him in his native State and several outside it, but he managed to stay a free man in Kansas. His saloon was accepted as the meeting place of Texas men coming up the trail with cattle. He had won the saloon in a game of poker. His brother Johnny was a weaker and, if possible, wilder version of himself. Fred was continually getting his younger brother out of scrapes.

Darcy now called to McAllister: "Mornin', friend."

McAllister crossed to him. As he drew

close, Darcy's eyes opened wide in recognition.

"Wa-al, if'n it ain't Rem McAllister." They shook. "How've you been, boy?"

They chatted of this and that, Darcy telling proudly of how well he was doing in this benighted northern town and what a pleasure it was to be making his pile from the hated Yankees. Which wasn't what McAllister had heard. It seemed that Darcy made most of his money from the cattlemen of Texas. Finally, Darcy said: "I heard Malloy was killed."

McAllister told him: "Two men walked into his office and cut down on him with a greener."

Darcy tapped McAllister's badge with a forefinger.

"That gives you a personal interest, I reckon."

"Sure does."

They were very casual about it, but tension came between the two of them. Darcy had treed more town marshals in his time than any other man alive.

"Ain't many Texas men town marshals, Rem. Not in Kansas."

"Ain't many Texas men had a friend shot down in front of their eyes, Fred."

They eyed each other like wary dogs.

"You get a good look at the men who did it?"

"I'd know 'em if they grew beards, I'd know them twenty years from now. And I'm goin' to find 'em."

Darcy laughed.

"You don't think them fellers stayed around here after doin' that. Hell, they'd be crazy."

"Maybe they did and maybe they didn't, but I'll find 'em."

There was a short silence and Remington added: "You know who did it, Fred?"

"No," Darcy said, "I don't have no idea."

McAllister knew he did. He started to go on, nodding his farewell.

"Come around and have a drink with me," Darcy invited.

"I'll take you up on that."

23

He walked the town, visited the stock-pens and the railroad spurs, walked through the smell of cattle, the dust and the bawling. A crowd of punchers with their long staffs with the pricker at the end were mouching near the line, men were driving cows aboard the train. McAllister turned away—this part of the cattle trade always sickened him a little. He didn't like to see the wild creatures who had run free on the prairies and in the brush being packed into wagons. He looked out over the prairie to the holding grounds and saw the thousands of cattle grazing and wondered when the north-ward flow of the newfound wealth of Texas would stop. Then he turned back toward the office, found a small café and went in for breakfast. He had just enough for ham, eggs, fried potatoes and coffee. He would have to ask Carson for some money or he'd starve.

He returned to the office and spent the day dozing at his desk. He wasn't a man who believed in action when it wasn't necessary and he hadn't made up his mind what he was going to do or even what he could do about Art Malloy. What he wanted to know was: had the men who had killed him come of their own accord or had they been sent? If they had been sent, any one of a half-dozen men could have sent them.

He had his eyes closed and his hat over them, chair tilted back and feet on desk when he heard the door to the street open softly. Before he could move he heard a female gasp of horror. He pushed his hat back, opened his eyes, let all four legs of the chair fall flat and took his feet from the desk.

In the center of the office stood a vision. Golden hair and blue eyes that were now wide with indignation, dress of green silk, bonnet bright with flowers. Her figure was superlative, slim waist and full breasts. She was maybe a couple of years older than he was.

"How can you sit there?" she demanded.

McAllister rose to his feet.

"Wa-al, ma'am, I bend my legs an' I—"

"And now you can joke."

"Ma'am?"

"Art Malloy has not been dead more than a few hours—"

"May I ask your name, ma'am?"

She drew herself up.

"I'm Miss Emily Penshurst."

"Any relation to the banker?"

"I'm his daughter."

"An' you were a friend of Art's?"

She sobered a little, but the indignation still showed in her fine eyes.

"I was a friend of his. Both my father and I were."

"Were you an' Art engaged to be married?"

She hesitated and McAllister interpreted that as meaning that though they had not been engaged there had been some sort of an understanding between them. He wondered if this was the lady Carson had mentioned.

"Do you know a man called Will Drummond?"

"Why, yes I do. Though what that has to do with—I don't know what your name is, sir, but I did not come here to answer questions, but to ask them." Her eyes flashed. McAllister reckoned Art must have had his hands full with this one. On second thoughts, he reckoned he wouldn't mind at all having his hands full of her.

"Ask 'em," he said.

"What do you intend to do about the killing of Art Malloy?"

"That's a fair question."

"Perhaps you'd be good enough to answer it."

"Sure. I intend to catch the men who did it and if I don't shoot them dead, I reckon they'll hang."

"That won't happen with you sitting here."

"It'll happen when I get around."

"Then I suggest you start."

"An' I suggest, ma'am, that you go about your business and quit teaching your grandmother how to suck eggs."

She started back at his rudeness.

27

"There's no call for you to be insulting. Mr. Malloy was a good friend of ours and—"

"It might interest you to know, ma'am, that Art was a good friend of mine, too. Never fear, Miss Penshurst, you'll get your murderers . . . on a plate."

"I wish I could believe that."

"Now perhaps you could tell me some more about Mr. Drummond."

"What has he to do with this?"

"That's what I'm tryin' to find out."

"I fail to see any connection."

"I didn't say there was one," McAllister told her. "I'm tryin' to find out if there was."

"I assure you that Will Drummond had nothing to do with Art Malloy's death."

"Maybe he didn't," McAllister said, "but I want to know all about everybody in this town that hated Art and there's a good few of them."

"What makes you think Mr. Drummond hated Art?" She looked a little frightened now, though the indignation was still there.

28

"Because Art was in love with you and you're very beautiful."

She flushed red and lowered her eyes.

"What makes you think Art was in love with me?"

"One look at you is enough to convince me."

She turned half away from him.

"I don't think I care for this conversation."

"Don't like it much myself. Now Drummond—did he ever show hate for Art?"

She hesitated again.

"He didn't like him. But that doesn't mean he hated him. Why, if you knew Will Drummond, you'd know that he wasn't capable of murder."

"Everybody is capable of murder, Miss Penshurst. To either do it or hire somebody to do it."

"Your suggestion is vile."

"Why did Drummond hate Art?"

The question hung for a moment between them. She clenched and unclenched her hands.

"I won't admit he hated him."

"Why did he dislike him, then?"

"I suppose—oh, I don't know. If you had known both men you'd have seen how different they were. They were opposites."

McAllister said: "The opposite to Art would be something pretty unpleasant. He was straight and he was honest."

"I know that. I didn't mean opposite in that way. I meant . . . it's not easy to say this, not with Art dead, but Will Drummond is a gentleman. He has nice manners, likes literature and the arts. Art wasn't like that. He was . . . rough."

"Art was the gentlest man I ever knew."

"It was the way he lived . . . with guns."

McAllister held his temper.

"All right, ma'am," he said, "you've said your piece and I get your drift. You want Art's killers caught and so do I. We agree. You go off to your sewing bee and leave the dirty work to men like me . . . and Art."

She gave him a look with some anguish in it then and he felt a little sorry he had said that, but not much.

"Very well," she said softly. She looked as if she'd say some more, but she didn't; she turned on her heel and walked out onto the street. He went to the door and watched her angling across to the bank. He walked back into the office and found that the air was full of the smell of her. It was pretty nice. Art could have been crazy about that girl and so could Drummond. Men had been killed over a woman like that before now.

3

IT was getting near to dark. Already in some of the buildings along Lincoln lamps were lit. McAllister sat outside the office smoking his pipe. He watched Jim Carson walking down the street from the hotel.

A wagon drew up, blocking his view of the bank entrance. Two cowhands rode past, giving him glances as they went. He was the law and if they were going to have fun in their own way they might be meeting up with him later.

Carson came up and said: "All quiet?"

"All quiet."

They walked into the office together.

"Going to make a start on finding Art's killer tonight," Carson said.

"Where do you start?" McAllister asked.

Carson buckled on his gun. Took a

bottle from a drawer, offered McAllister a drink, was refused and took one himself.

"The Darcy boys is as good a start as any."

"Fred's tough."

"Don't I know it."

They both swung around as a dull explosion came to their ears. McAllister jumped for the door with Carson close behind him. A shot came from the direction of the bank. Carson pushed McAllister forward and ran onto the street, gun in hand. At once a rifle opened fire from the opposite side of the street, lead hummed past them both and a window of the office collapsed with a crash of broken glass. They both turned and dove back into the office, knowing they couldn't survive out there. Carson got to a window and stared out across the street.

"They're cleanin' out the bank," he said needlessly.

McAllister said: "Get yourself a rifle and cut down anybody that comes out of there. I'm goin' around the rear."

He found his Henry, checked the loads

and went out of the rear door of the office. He turned right, ran along the back of the buildings and went on along an alleyway between two stores that brought him out opposite the bank. At once he was shot at and was driven further back down the alley. Whoever was pulling this job were surely well-organised. They had all points covered.

He could see now that the light wagon in front of the bank was turned on its side and guessed that at least one marksman was hiding behind it. He could see no one moving about inside the bank. There was nothing to shoot at. From up the street there came shouts. From the office came the sound of shots. Carson was doing his best. The answering fire McAllister saw came from the roof of the bank. He waited, knowing that soon or late a man would have to show himself.

After a few minutes, he heard a shrill whistle.

A man burst suddenly from behind the upturned wagon and started for the alleyway at the side of the bank. The

Henry's butt was in McAllister's shoulder, he aimed hastily and fired. The shot hit the man and drove him running against the wall of a building. But he went on and was quickly lost to view.

McAllister ran out of the alleyway.

No shot came from the direction of the bank. He crossed the street to the mouth of the alley running alongside the bank. From the other end of the alley came shouts; his eye caught a flurry of movement, men moving around, horses turning. Several shots came in his direction and he flung himself flat on the ground. Feet pounded behind him and Carson arrived. Shots drove him away from the mouth of the alley to shelter behind the bank itself.

The shooting stopped and horses' hoofs pounded. McAllister lurched to his feet. He needed a horse and quick. Full darkness would be here in a moment and the robbers would get clear under its cover. He turned and ran for the saloon. There were several men outside it now.

"I want a horse," McAllister shouted.

They merely stared at him. Carson came up, panting.

"Take any horse you want," he cried. He untied a sorrel and a man came forward hastily.

"Get your hands off my horse," he bellowed.

"The city's requisitioning it," Carson told him.

"The city'll pay if any harm comes to him."

McAllister turned to a chunky bay, untied it and vaulted into the saddle. As he turned away from the hitching rail, a man yelled for him to stop. He raked home the spurs and the animal hit a flat run down the street. Carson was close behind him. A moment later they ran neck and neck out of the town onto the eastering road.

"There they go," Carson cried.

McAllister saw a dark bunch of horsemen going fast over the first ridge.

They came to the creek and splashed into it, sending up a cloud of wild spray. The horses came out dripping on the further side and climbed the bank, the two riders spurring them as they went.

As they came into view of the plain above, McAllister thought he heard a distant shot over the sound of the horses' hoofs. The bay seemed to take a leap in the air. When it came down it landed on legs of paper and McAllister scarcely had time to kick his feet from the stirrup-irons and jump clear. He picked himself up and the horse lay screaming and kicking. McAllister ducked under several shots that came his way, shot the horse through the head and got down behind it.

Carson had reined around and was pounding back to McAllister. To go further along the road was impossible. His horse halted and he jumped from the saddle to join McAllister. They peered along the road but there was little they could see. It was almost full dark now. The bank-raiders had carefully chosen their time to make their attack. The two lawmen heard the distant and dying sound of hoof-beats, but McAllister reckoned there were still at least two men guarding the road.

Full dark swooped down on them.

McAllister said: "We ain't doin' no good here. Let's get back to town."

They stood up. Nothing happened. McAllister fought the saddle and bridle off the dead horse and Carson said: "You would have to get that horse shot. Now there'll be hell to pay when we get back to town."

"What was I supposed to do," McAllister wanted to know, "let those jaspers get away?"

Carson laughed ruefully.

"They did that any road. No, I know this town. Likely you'll pay for the nag out of your own pocket."

McAllister said something choicely obscene. They both climbed onto the sorrel and, laden with the saddle, they headed back for town. They felt a mite foolish.

An hour later, they returned to their office. A fair amount had happened in that hour—the mayor had said the town would pay for the horse when McAllister threatened to resign; the banker, Penshurst, a fussy little man had wept and declared that he was ruined. The robbers had got clean away with twenty thousand dollars in gold. The two marshals made coffee, laced it strongly with whiskey and sat at their desks sipping it.

Carson said: "This is a damned good start. Art killed dead and now the bank raided. Maybe there's a jinx on our partnership."

"Ever have a hunch?" McAllister asked.

"Plenty."

"I have a hunch Art being killed and this raid are connected."

Carson lit a stogie and puffed.

"I can't see that," he said.

"Nor can I," McAllister agreed, "but that's my hunch. There's a little reason behind it when you look at it. This town was afraid of Art. More afraid than of you an' me. Would anybody have dared make that raid if Art was alive?"

"Makes sense," Carson had to agree. "I reckon if'n you find those raiders you'll find Art's killers."

Carson stood up.

"I'll patrol around a bit an' try to make the town afraid of *me*," he said.

McAllister said: "I'll stick around for another couple of hours, then I'll hit the hay. Leave the Darcys to me, will you, Jim?"

Carson looked at him for a moment.

"Sure," he said. "But they're poison."

He went out.

McAllister checked the old Remington, stood thinking for a moment and followed him onto the street. He walked along to the Golden Fleece and entered. The place was full to bursting point, the din was deafening and it looked like business had never been better. He found the two Darcys together at the bar, drinking whiskey.

Johnny Darcy was smaller than his brother, but very like him with the same deceptive sober air. Both brothers greeted McAllister effusively, clapped him on the back and declared that he must drink with them. He accepted. They drank, they talked of old times in Texas, McAllister heard again how the brothers Darcy were coming up in the world and were making money. Finally, McAllister said: "Somewhere I can talk to you two boys in private?"

"Sure," said Fred, "Come on into the office."

They pushed their way through the crowd to a side room, full of plush chairs, a rolltop desk and scattered papers.

"Have another drink, Rem," Johnny said.

"Not now, Johnny, thanks."

They turned and faced him, both alert to his change of tone.

"What's eatin' you, Rem?" Fred demanded.

McAllister said: "When something pretty rough happened in this town, Art Malloy always used to pay you two a visit."

Johnny said: "Art was a Yankee and he didn't like us Texans."

41

Fred laughed.

"But you don't feel like that, Rem boy. You're one of us."

"I'm a marshal of this town, Fred, and two pretty rough things have happened. One Art's been shot and two the bank's been raided. So I'm payin' you two a visit."

They looked aghast.

"You can't mean it," Fred exclaimed.

"I don't mean nothin'—yet. I'm just askin' questions."

"What questions?"

"Did you have anything to do with either?"

Fred spread his hands. "Does it make sense, Rem. Hell, we've all the money in the world. An' Art wasn't doin' us no harm."

"You had a run in a short time back."

"Didn't mean a thing, Rem," said Johnny. "Not a damn thing."

McAllister used a moment of silence, while the two men eyed him. Finally, the marshal said: "I recognised the man that shot Art."

That shook them.

"Who was it?" Fred demanded.

"A man you used to run with way back."

"Who was it?"

"You sure you don't know, Fred?"

"I'd swear it on a stack of Bibles."

"It was Frank Little."

Both men looked amazed and Fred whispered: "Ace Reno!"

Johnny said: "Frank could be bought for a dollar. You think we hired him?"

"It's a possibility."

Anger touched the elder brother now.

"We don't have to stand this kind of talk from you or any other man, McAllister," he shouted.

McAllister smiled.

"I'll be around again, Fred, an' I'll be askin' more questions. You two boys had best get your stories straight."

He turned to the door and walked out. As he went through the doorway the muscles in his back crept a little when he thought of what the Darcys were capable of.

He elbowed his way through the crowded saloon and was glad to breath the fresh air of the street. That left Fritz Commer of the Longhorns, Will Drummond and Wild Jack Little's brothers.

He stopped a passerby.

"You know a man named Will Drummond?"

"Who don't?"

"Where does he live?"

"Last house of the last block on Garrett."

"Thanks."

He walked down Lincoln. It was busy with evening strollers. It was a warm pleasant evening. He turned down Garrett not hurrying and at last came to a pleasant house set among trees and with a white picket fence surrounding it. He opened the gate and stepped into a front yard which was fragrant with flowers. The light of lamps showed in the windows. He rapped on the front door with his quirt butt. A moment later it was opened by a middle-aged woman with a stern face.

"Mr. Drummond?"

44

"Well, sir, he's entertaining at the moment."

"I'd like a minute of his time if he can spare it."

Her eyes were on his badge.

"Who shall I say?"

"McAllister—town marshal."

She hesitated, not knowing whether to invite him in or not. She apparently decided not, for she went into the house leaving him standing there. A moment later, a man several years older than McAllister appeared. He wore a good brown suit, highly polished shoes and a neat necktie. His hair was sleek and there was an altogether gentleness about him, though he gave the impression of some strength. There might be a gentleness there, but there was no weakness. His features were good, the hair fair, the mustache had the fullness that was then fashionable. So this gentleman had been Art's rival. No wonder poor old Art had been in trouble. This kind of man would appeal to a woman like Emily Penshurst.

"Mr. McAllister, we haven't met. I

believe you're the new town marshal." He extended a hand and they shook. Drummond's handshake was firm.

"I'm just moseying around town asking questions, Mr. Drummond."

"What about?"

"Art Malloy's death."

"I should have guessed. A terrible thing."

"You didn't like Art."

"I—" The direct statement had taken the wind out of his sails. "I imagine there were plenty of people who didn't like him."

"But not as much as you."

The directness of that statement seemed to take him aback too.

"Whatever makes you say that?"

"You had good personal reasons for not liking him. I'd put it stronger than that. I suggest you hated him."

Drummond's face flushed with anger.

"See here, you can't come here and talk this way on my own doorstep. I have guests. You don't know this town and I am willing to make allowances for your

46

ignorance. Maybe you don't know that I'm a man of some standing here."

McAllister said: "I don't give a monkey's damn if'n you're the emperor of China. All I know is you hated Art and you'd of liked to see him dead."

"Nothing could be further from the truth. I didn't like the man, but that doesn't mean that I hated him and wanted him dead."

"Mr. Drummond, I've seen the lady."

"What lady?"

"The one who was the reason for you hating Art."

For a moment it looked as if Drummond couldn't believe his ears. Then he shouted: "Why, you—" and looked to be about to strike McAllister.

McAllister said with a quick grin: "Lay a finger on me and I'll take you in, boy."

That stopped Drummond. McAllister was satisfied—he had gotten to the man's elemental self straight off.

"McAllister," Drummond said through his teeth, "If I ever hear you mention that lady's name, I'll—"

47

"Come after me with a shotgun from behind?"

Drummond went white. He stared at McAllister for a moment, seemed to collect himself a little and said: "Are you accusing me of killing Malloy, McAllister?"

"Whatever gave you that idea?" McAllister asked. "I'm just asking around."

"McAllister, there were plenty of men who wanted Malloy dead. Search among the riffraff of this town, not among the respectable. Now, if you'll excuse me, I'll return to my guests."

"Sure, I'll excuse you."

McAllister strolled down the path and went out of the gateway. When he looked back, Drummond was still staring at him from the open doorway.

It was a fine night. McAllister strolled along Garrett, reached the intersection and went west along Main. At the end of Main was a blacksmith's shop. McAllister stooped at the doorway and went in. The smith was busy at the anvil beating out shoes for a good sorrel horse that stood

48

there. At the bellows was a boy. The smith was a giant of a man, all bulging muscles, sweat and tangled hair. McAllister waited patiently until the man had finished and fitted the shoe. The boy led the horse out into the yard.

McAllister said: "McAllister, deputy-marshal."

"Clem Malloy."

McAllister raised his eyebrows. "Didn't know Art had a brother."

"Cousin."

"Know who killed him?"

"Wish to God I did."

"Clem, where was you at when the bank was raided today?"

"Right here."

McAllister went on: "How long were you here after the raid?"

"All morning."

"Any riders come in from the west, hour-two hours after the raid?"

The giant frowned. Finally, he said: "Yeah. Two-three horsebackers come in. Usual farm wagons too."

49

"The horsebackers—did they come in together or separately?"

"Separately."

"Know 'em?"

Again the frown. "One of 'em. Feller called Ranshaw. Don't recollect his other name."

"Thanks, Clem."

"You goin' to get Art's killer, McAllister?"

"Do my best."

"Anything I can do to help. You call on me."

"I'll do that."

McAllister walked out onto the street, feeling that he had an ally there. *Ranshaw*, he thought—it could be a lead. There was just a faint chance. The fact that a horseman had ridden into town from the west while the raiders had disappeared into the east could mean nothing at all, but he was riding one of his hunches.

Almost opposite the blacksmith's was a gunsmith's. He crossed and went in. The gunsmith was a little man of middle years with a bald head and steel-rimmed spectacles. They exchanged greetings and McAllister asked him where he had been when the raid on the bank took place. The man replied that he had been at his home, a block away. When the shooting had started, he had run to see what it was all about. He had watched the raid from a safe distance, then, when the raiders rode off from the rear of the bank he had stood around talking with folks for awhile and come here to his shop.

"Anybody you know ride in from the west during the morning?" McAllister asked.

The little man looked a little surprised at the question, but he said quickly enough: "Sure, several."

"Could you name 'em?"

"One was George Ranshaw. I remember him clearly. He spoke to me."

"Could you name the others?"

"Sure. There was Johnny Dikes, Hat Palmer, Sven Carlson, Lew Goad and, let me see now, Burt Evans."

"Any of those farmers?"

51

"Carlson and Goad."

"Thanks."

"You're welcome. You goin' to get the man that killed Art Malloy, marshal?"

"Sure."

"Good man." The little man adjusted his spectacles and added: "They don't come any better'n Art Malloy."

McAllister strolled down Main, across the intersection and came on Jim Carson standing outside the Longhorns.

"You got trouble in there, Jim?"

"Fight, but it seems to of quietened down now."

Just then a shot sounded.

McAllister said: "Here's your chance to impress the town."

Carson gave him a look that carried some worry in it. But he wasn't scared. Art Malloy wouldn't have employed a deputy who scared easily. Carson shouldered his way into the saloon. McAllister waited where he was for a moment, heard Carson's voice and slipped inside when he knew that all eyes would be on Carson. The marshal was in the middle of the floor. Not far from him lay a man, one leg feebly kicking. Two bouncers hovered in the background, held back by the gun in the hand of a cowman who stood near the bar. Carson was telling this man to hand over his gun.

"I got friends here, lawman," the drover was saying, "you get the hell outa here, crawl into your hole and pull it in after you."

Carson hesitated to pull a gun while one pointed at his midriff.

"Quit acting like a fool," he said. "I'm takin' you in."

Several members of the crowd told him what he could do with himself. McAllister slipped his old Remington from its holster, stepped into the open to one side of the cowhand and said: "You're mutton, Texas."

The boy gaped at him. Carson drew his gun. The boy's eyes shifted from one lawman to the other.

"It takes two of you," he said bitterly.

McAllister stepped up to him and took his gun from his hand, stuffing it under his own belt. He took a look at the man on the ground and saw that he had been drilled clean between the eyes.

Carson asked: "What happened?"

A man nearby said: "The kid done what any other man would of done. This feller cut down on him. His gun was cocked afore the kid drew."

"Any more witnesses?" Carson asked. There were several. "Walk down to my office and we'll put it down in writing. Lock the kid up, Rem. Charge him with being in possession of a firearm."

They all trooped down to the office, the boy was locked in the cell which McAllister had been in so short a time before, the men gave their evidence and Carson wrote it down. It was an hour before only the two lawmen were left alone in the office.

McAllister and Carson took a drink.

"Jim, I have some names. Tell me what you can about them," McAllister said.

"Shoot."

"George Ranshaw."

"No visible means of support, except cards and a gun. Do you?"

"Fine. Point him out to me later."

"You're supposed to be off duty."

"I'm working my way toward the men that raided the bank. And the men that killed Art Malloy."

"You have a hunch?"

"That's about all I have. Johnny Dikes."

"Works around the stock-pens. Young. Nice kid."

"Why should he ride into town from the west of a morning?"

"Courtin' a girl out that away. Sees her any excuse he can."

"Hat Palmer."

"No good. Runs with the Darcy boys. Kansas man. I suspect he rides with the men raiding the Texas herds. He cut the throat of a man right here in town and got away with self-defense."

"Burt Evans."

"A bad hat, but a cut above the average. Fast with a gun. Has somethin' of a reputation. He's a dresser and he

55

always seems to have money, though I never learned where he got it." Carson looked at McAllister curiously. "You think these boys had somethin' to do with killing Art and carryin' out the raid."

"The raid. I know who did the killin'. Point these fellers out to me, Jim."

Carson rose. "Sure, do it now. You want some help."

"I'll tell you when I do."

Carson walked to the door and turned. "You think they carried out the raid and returned to town? Rem, you could be gettin' yourself into a heap of trouble. Any one of those men would kill you for a dollar."

"Maybe it would be a good thing if they tried. We'd nail 'em then."

Carson smiled. "Rather you than me."

They walked down the street to the Golden Fleece and shouldered their way inside. The place was as crowded as usual at that time of the night. The noise was deafening, the air thick with smoke. They pushed their way through the crowd and reached the bar. Carson took a good look around.

"Burt Evans at the table there to the left. Tall man with sideboards and black mustache."

McAllister looked at the man. He was in his early thirties, immaculately dressed in clawhammer coat and silk vest. His face was narrow and handsome. He was smiling and showing strong white teeth. McAllister summed him up as having plenty of sand, but of being vain. He wondered how quickly he would break. He reckoned he would soon find out.

"You want some help?" Carson asked.

"Just keep the others off'n my back," McAllister said and stepped forward.

He went forward until he stood beside the man. Evans flicked him a glance and said: "I don't like anybody overlooking my cards, friend."

"I'm not looking at your cards," McAllister told him, "and I'm not your friend."

The man laid his cards down and stared up at the tall man.

"Ah," he exclaimed in cultured tones, "the new deputy, boys. What can I do for you, marshal?"

"Step down to the office for a word."

"I'm busy right now and I have no secrets. Talk freely before these gentlemen."

"Right. You ain't allowed to carry guns in this town and you have one."

The man went rigid.

"Do you aim to take it from me?"

"That's the general idea."

"Then I shall give it to you."

The right hand flicked quick as the head of a spitting snake and a small vest-pocket gun appeared in it. The men at the table dove away, but the shot never came. McAllister's own right hand also moved with speed and, clenched, it struck Evans in the side of the neck. Even as he fell sideways, McAllister's left hand crossed over and took the deadly little pistol from the man's hand. Evans went sideways and hit the floor hard. McAllister dropped the pistol into his pocket, kicked the chair aside and stood over the fallen man.

Carson, gun in hand, said: "Stand back and let the man have air, boys." The whole place went still.

Holding his neck, his face grimacing with pain, Evans staggered to his feet. He looked like a considerably shaken man.

McAllister said: "I'm arrestin' you for carrying concealed weapons and for assaultin' a peace officer. Comin' peaceable?"

With a strangled cry of rage, Evans launched himself at the deputy. That right hand of his moved again as he leapt and a short knife appeared in it. McAllister kicked the chair again and Evans fell over it. As he went down McAllister lifted a blow from his belt level, catching Evans on the side of the head. The man hit the planks and lay still. Somebody whistled their appreciation. McAllister took Evans by the collar of his fine coat and dragged him away from the table. Men made a way for him and McAllister dragged him through the door and out onto the sidewalk. By the time McAllister had tossed him onto the street, he had started to come around. The men who had followed them onto the sidewalk watched him get to his feet. Suddenly he looked frail and weak.

McAllister said: "Walk ahead of me to the jail. Make a break and I'll shoot you in the leg. I'd like that."

The man started to walk. His legs seemed to be made of paper. By the time they reached the jail the fresh air had helped to revive him. Inside the office, Evans took one look at the iron grill of the jail and wilted again.

"You're not going to lock me up," he said, "nobody ever did that."

"First time for everythin'," McAllister said. "Sit down before you fall down."

The trail-driver came to the grill and watched them with interest.

Evans sat down.

McAllister said: "Why'd you ride in from west of town this mornin'?"

The man looked startled.

"What in hell does that have to do with

60

me carrying a gun and assaulting a peace officer?"

"Nothin'. Answer the question."

"I went for a ride."

"Good answer. Only it ain't the truth and I'm goin' to have the truth from you, Evans. An' I'm goin' to have it quick. I just naturally hate to sit around jawin' with a coyote like you."

"I'm telling you the truth."

McAllister said: "Look, Evans, either you talk or any minute now you're goin' to assault me again and I'm goin' to beat the livin' daylights outa you."

Evans looked enraged.

"That's more than you dare do, McAllister. That boy there's a witness. You heard him threaten me, son."

McAllister laughed, which should have been warning enough.

"Mister," he said, "that boy just killed a man in self-defense. Come mornin' he'll walk outa here after payin' a ten-dollar fine. An' he don't like Yankee trash like you any more'n I do." He turned to the boy. "That right, son?"

"Sure thing, marshal."

McAllister turned to Evans, smiling blandly.

4

FRED DARCY turned to his brother as soon as McAllister had dragged the unfortunate Evans from the Golden Fleece and said: "Look after the place, boy, I got urgent business."

Johnny Darcy said: "If Evans talks we could end up with rope collars."

Fred cursed. "You're tellin' me. It was the craziest thing I ever heard, pulling this thing and getting back here in town."

"Let me go settle Evans. Evans and McAllister both."

"You stay still, kid, hear? You'n'me come out of this with a whole skin. There're hired guns to do this kind of work."

Fred walked along the bar, let himself out of a side entrance into an alleyway and reached the backlots. He kept to the shadows until he was near the intersection with Garrett, hurried across Main and

63

entered the backlots behind Garrett. He was nervous, not only because he didn't want to be seen on the streets by Carson and McAllister, but because he wanted to approach the man he was going to see without the knowledge of his housekeeper.

He knew that he had reached the house he wanted when he saw the white picket fence in the glooming. He stepped over it and approached the house. Peering through the window, he saw the housekeeper sitting at the table in the kitchen. He went around to the front of the house and peeked in at the parlor window. Here he saw Penshurst, the banker, and his daughter. Sitting opposite them, chatting pleasantly was the man he had come to see—Drummond.

Rack his brains as he might, he could think of no way of speaking to Drummond without calling attention to himself, so he decided to take a risk and knock on the front door. He did this and the housekeeper answered his knock. By the look on her face he could see that he was not approved of.

"I'd like a word with Mr. Drummond, ma'am."

'I'm afraid he's entertaining at the moment."

Darcy tried some of his Texas charm. "I can't say how sorry I am to bother you, ma'am. But this is a matter of the greatest urgency."

She hesitated, then she said: "I'll tell Mr. Drummond."

Darcy waited, worrying. He wasn't scared of Drummond, he told himself. He wasn't scared of any man living. What was there about Drummond that made him uneasy? The man was soft-handed, he wasn't any hand with a gun, he was a Northerner. But his brain was clear, he possessed a cool daring which aroused the admiration of the Texan and he was utterly ruthless. He was also a gentleman, a status that puzzled Darcy.

Drummond appeared. At the sight of Darcy his face went white and set. He came close to the Texan and spoke in a low voice through his teeth.

"I thought I told you never to contact me direct," he said.

Darcy didn't like the tone. He was his own master and he didn't like being treated like a servant.

"You think I'd of come if it wasn't urgent?"

"What happened?"

"McAllister took Burt Evans."

"What?"

Drummond was aghast. Darcy never would have thought to see the man so shaken.

"Walked into my place and suckered him," Darcy said. "Knocked seven different kinds of hell outa him and dragged him off to the calaboose."

"Didn't Evans have a gun on him?" Drummond demanded.

"McAllister took it from him like a feller takin' candy from a kid. Never seen anything like it." He lowered his voice. "Drummond, we want McAllister dead, fast. And I'm the man to do it."

"Not you, Fred," Drummond told him.

"I'm fast enough."

"I'm sure you are. But we need you for other work. I'll handle this. Leave it with me."

"All right. Make it good, Drummond. We have a sweet set-up here and we don't want it spoiled," Darcy said.

"I've managed matters to your satisfaction, haven't I?" Drummond asked.

Darcy grinned a little.

"Sure thing. I don't have any grumbles."

"Anybody see you home here."

"Nary a one, except that woman of yourn."

"She won't talk."

"See you."

Darcy hurried away along the side of the house and disappeared into the darkness. Drummond stood for a moment deep in thought, before he went back into the house, a pleasant smile set on his face for the benefit of his guests.

As he entered the room, the girl at the table looked up with a smile.

"You're greatly in demand tonight," she said.

He shrugged ruefully.

"Always business," he said. "One could hanker after being a failure sometimes."

The banker stared at him like a man in shock, envying the younger man, knowing that his own life had come to an end. He was finished financially. It would take a miracle to put him on his feet again. He had been struck a low in a few minutes of time that had hurled him from a position of power and respect to one of failure and poverty. Always a confident man, he suddenly lacked all confidence. He had lost twenty thousand dollars belonging to the business men of this community. First thing in the morning he would get on the wire and see how many of his so-called friends in the banking world would rally to his aid. When he recovered himself sufficiently. Just for now he would try and relax here drinking Drummond's good wine, try to get some warmth back into his chilled body. Drummond was being more attentive than usual to his daughter. Of course, if the two of them married . . .

They were laughing and talking together. How Emily could laugh at a time like this, he couldn't fathom. She must be harder than he thought her. Maybe, of course, if she were really her father's daughter, as he suspected she was, she might be playing Drummond on the end of a line. He had suspected that she had been fond of that Art Malloy fellow, but her head had ruled against her heart. With Drummond, she would have everything.

He jerked himself to attention. Drummond was talking to him.

". . . I don't want you to feel too badly, sir. All is not lost. The situation has come upon me suddenly and I have not thought my way through it yet, but I am sure when we have talked it over that some solution can be found."

The banker's voice was shaking when he spoke—

"What do you mean exactly?"

Drummond laughed lightly.

"That's what I'm saying, sir," he said. "I can't say *exactly* what I mean. But I feel sure we can come to some arrangement. I have money lying idle and I detest idle money. I don't know how much precisely, but there is a fair amount. We'll have a talk soon."

"If you're talking," Penshurst said, "about the bank going into liquidation, I shall be wiring friends in the morning to see what help I can raise."

"No need for that," Drummond said largely. "I mean, let's try and keep it in the family, as it were." Emily blushed and smiled at him. "We'll talk in the morning. How does that suit you?"

"If you have any hope to offer," the banker said, "it suits me very well."

Drummond's hand was resting on his daughter's and Emily had not taken hers away. Perhaps this was the miracle Penshurst had been hoping for.

Later that evening, when his guests had departed, Drummond put his head into the kitchen. The housekeeper raised her head.

"What did that man Darcy want?" she demanded.

Drummond told her. She swore like a man.

"You'll have to do something and damned quick," she told him.

"I intend to."

"You'll have to kill Evans and McAllister, you know."

"Evans is our immediate worry."

"They'll be taking him in front of the judge tomorrow at ten. Both men could be killed then."

"We'll see."

"There mustn't be any seeing about it. Kill 'em both and have done."

Drummond protested: "There could be real risk in killing a marshal."

"You killed Malloy and there was no risk to it."

"That's not true. McAllister's sniffing at the truth now. He's shown that by taking in Evans."

"That was for the bank I'll bet. Any

road, it proves we want McAllister dead even more. Do it, boy, or you'll regret it, mark my words."

"All right, I'll try."

He shut the door and walked into the parlor. From the drawer of a bureau he took a pocket Remington and slipped it under his belt. His coat covered it to perfection, but the butt was within easy access of his right hand. He went out of the house through the kitchen without another word to the woman and made his way through the backlots to the edge of town. Here was timber and brush. He picked his way carefully through this so that he would not get his clothes torn or his boots muddy, till he came to a shack hidden among the trees.

He hailed it from a distance because he knew the men inside were jumpy. He had taught them to be that way. He was annoyed at having to come here at all, because he hated having to contact these men. These were the laborers and he despised them. Though some of them were efficient enough, a few of them masters of their craft. At his hail some-body inside dimmed the light. There came the sound of the door opening.

A man's voice called—

"Who is this?"

"The boss."

No names.

"Come ahead."

He approached the shack and entered. A hand turned up the lamp. He glanced around at the untidy interior, the bunks and their disheveled blankets, the dirty crockery, the bottles and cans lying around on the floor. The place smelled of unwashed bodies and foul tobacco. Whenever he came here, he wanted to retch, to take a bath. They lived like the pigs they were.

Marve and Frank Little were at the table playing cards. They watched him now and having their eyes on him made him squirm. They were like animals and their eyes were without feeling. There were maybe a half dozen men there and they were of the same breed, but none of them were in the same class with the two brothers.

"Evening, men," Drummond said.

They murmured a reply. The Little brothers said nothing. They just stared at him.

"Marve, Frank, I'd like a word with you outside," he said.

They considered that, as though there was a possibility of their not going. Then slowly, they put down their cards and strolled slowly to the door. Outside they turned and waited for him. He shut the door and turned to them.

"McAllister took Burt Evans," he told them.

They said nothing. Marve sneered a little. They were tall rangy man, built on the lean side. They were good hands with horses, but better hands with guns. Mercy was a word foreign to them. They liked fast horses, drink, women and easy money.

"Evans talks," he said, "and we could all hang. You two first."

Frank said: "Evans won't talk so easy."

He lisped a little because his front teeth were missing.

"McAllister's an Indian," Marve said. "He's no Malloy. He'll make Evans talk."

"So I want Evans dead."

"And McAllister?"

"Dead too. But Evans is your first target."

"We ain't agreed to no target yet," Marve said.

"It's in your own interests," Drummond said. "Any day now, McAllister's coming after you."

Frank said: "We could ride."

Drummond was prepared for this eventuality. He'd tried to gain his objective cheaply and failed. Now he would dicker about the price.

He said: "You boys don't think I meant you to do this for nothing, did you? I'll arrange for the money owing to you and for fifty extra dollars each to be paid into my bank in El Paso."

As Drummond knew one of them would say, Marve said: "Not enough."

"Two hundred," Frank said.

"I can find somebody else," Drummond told them.

"Hunnerd and fifty," Marve offered.

"One hundred extra each and that's final," Drummond said.

They nodded and Marve said: "Fifty each now for expenses." That was the figure that Drummond had decided in his own mind. He was pleased.

"Done," he said. He took two rolls of notes from his pockets and handed them to the brothers. They stuffed them carelessly into their clothes as if they were worthless paper. Drummond shuddered. He went on: "McAllister or Carson will take Evans in front of the judge around ten tomorrow most likely. That should be your best chance. If you can't get McAllister, don't hang around. Evans is the one we have to have dead."

Marve said, his voice deadly: "Play it straight, Drummond. That money had better be in El Paso when we get there."

Drummond said: "I never welched in my life."

"There's always a first time."

"Do you have fast horses?"

"Best in the country."

"Fresh?"

"Raring to go."

"Good. I'll wish you luck, boys." None of them offered their hands. Drummond could not have touched either man. He nodded, turned on his heel and walked away. Marve spat. Frank laughed softly.

Frank said: "It surely tempts a man to take that bastard and clean this place out."

Marve said: "His kind make me sick to the stomach. You know that, Frank? He looked at us like we was dirt."

"How do we do it in the mornin'? Two rifles?"

"One'll do it. One of us with the horses. If McAllister ain't dead, we'll need to be movin' and then some."

"That canelo of his is sure fast."

"Nothin' ain't as fast as our two beauties."

"Highest card does the shootin'."
"Suits me."
They strolled back into the shack.

5

McALLISTER knocked out his pipe and stood up. Carson was cleaning his boots. They had decided that they would both guard Evans on the short trip to the judge's court in the Golden Fleece. McAllister loved the irony of court being held there. But it spelled real danger. Evans was important and the men behind him couldn't afford for him to talk. Neither marshal fooled himself that there could be more violence in the offing.

McAllister stood considering the matter of weapons. If anybody wanted Evans dead, they would want to remain safe themselves. That meant a rifle. Every rooftop and window was a potential danger spot. Both men would have to watch front, back, sides and upward as well. A dozen marshals could not have done the job properly. They had argued over swearing some more deputies in for the morning, but had decided against it. A handful of undisciplined guns could have added to their troubles.

"And," Carson said, "maybe they won't just be gunning for Evans. If they feel we're pushin' 'em, they would like to see us dead too."

McAllister laughed and the laugh didn't sound too good.

"You're in a real gay mood this morning," he said.

He decided on the Henry as against a greener. He knew the Henry and what it was capable of.

After some more argument, Carson thought that the opposition might not want Evans dead. Maybe they looked after their own and would try to get him out alive. In that case, he favored a scattergun.

"Quicker, cheaper and safer to have him dead," was McAllister's opinion and not for the first time he wished he were hunting bear in the Rockies, or roping wild longhorns in the brush—some safe occupation more to his liking.

Evans' attorney, Thomas Keene, a pale young man with ambition, arrived to see if his client was well and had not been knocked about. He talked with Evans for five minutes with their faces against the grill, then Keene left with a look of distaste for the two lawmen. It didn't trouble them unduly.

"Time to go," Carson said, found the keys and unlocked the cell door. Evans stepped out. He looked pale. He hadn't shaved because they hadn't allowed him a razor. This gave him an unkempt look that was not in character. This morning, he was very frightened.

McAllister picked up the Henry and said: "Feel like talking before we go, Evans? Either about Art or the robbery?"

"I don't know what you're talking about," the man said. His voice shook.

Carson clicked the irons on his wrists so that his hands were behind his back. Both lawmen were tense and knew it. Carson poured two drinks and he and

McAllister drank. Evans ran a thirsty tongue over his lips. His eyes were starting to look a little wild.

Carson smiled a little.

"Bring up the rear, Rem," he said. "An' you'd best walk backward."

He went out onto the street and looked around. There was a fair amount of foot and wheeled traffic about. He lifted a hand and McAllister said to the prisoner: "Get movin'." Evans hung back a moment, but McAllister gave him a shove and he walked uncertainly out onto the street. Once there, he looked around nervously. His tongue was still busy on his dry lips.

Carson started walking. McAllister prodded Evans after him and walked close behind him. As soon as he was out on the street, the flesh of his back crept in apprehension. His unfailing instinct told him that what was coming was coming soon. It would come before they reached the judge.

People were turning to stare now. They

had heard of the run in at the Golden
Fleece the night before.

Marve and Frank Little halted their
horses.

They were on a backlot.

Frank dismounted from his beautiful
black gelding and patted its shining neck
with genuine affection. He looked around
and he didn't like what he saw. He hadn't
thought of the trash lying around when
he had said for Marve to hold the horses
here.

"They could break a leg with all this
stuff around," he said.

Marve agreed.

"I could bring 'em right out on the
street," he said.

Frank shook his head.

"Could be lead flyin'," he said. "They
might get hit." He walked to the head of
the alleyway running between the buildings and leading to the street. Here to his
right was the rear of the hotel. The way
was clearer here. They could run directly

south from here. That might be better all around. "Bring 'em over here," he called.

Marve scooped up the black's dragging line and rode his superb bay over to where Frank stood. The elder brother heaved his rifle from the boot on the saddle, checked it and said: "Keno."

"Luck," Marve said and Frank walked away down the alley.

There was a water-butt almost on the street and Frank took his station here, buried in deep sun-shadow. He was slightly put-off to realise that the sun was against him here. A man coming down the street would have an advantage over him in this position. He cursed himself for not having thought of that before. He thought. He would take the risk of letting the prisoner and guard go past him. He'd catch Evans just as he was going into the Golden Fleece. It would be a slightly longer shot, but it was still an easy one for him.

He put his rifle behind the butt and rolled himself a smoke. Striking a lucifer on the seat of his pants, he puffed calmly.

He was a little tense, he discovered, but not unduly excited. There was real risk in this, he didn't deny, but he was a man almost without nerves. Odds didn't throw him, because he had supreme confidence in the speed of his own reactions. He didn't doubt that, all things being equal, he could kill prisoner and a guard with two shots. Then he'd leg it down the alley and away. The hard ride to El Paso, dodging the law and Indians all the way, keeping out of the sight of any living soul except when they obtained the necessary supplies. Then over the Border. They'd have a lot of fun in Mexico, him and Marve. They'd have money in their pockets.

He finished the smoke, dropped it and ground it out under his heel.

Folks were turning and looking up the street.

He put out his hand and touched the barrel of the rifle. The time was near.

The corner of the building to his right, obscured his view of the street and he didn't want to show himself by stepping forward for a clearer view. So he waited. A half-minute passed before Carson, the marshal, came into view. The man looked like he had troubles. He bore a six-shooter on his right hip and a greener in his hands held across his body, ready for action. Frank grinned wolfishly. That wouldn't do him good at the range he would start shooting.

Evans came into view, walking a good half-dozen paces behind the marshal. Behind him loomed McAllister's tall figure. Frank cursed. Trust that sonova-bitch to be close in that way. Unless Frank got Evans at just the right angle, it would be terribly difficult to make the shot. He might be forced to cut McAllister down first. The prisoner and his escort had to walk across the head of the alley, go a hundred paces to Frank's left before they turned into the Golden Fleece. As the line of men came broadside on to Frank, that was the moment for the gunman to shoot. The only time. McAllister being so close cut down the time available considerably. Now, if a townsman got in the way, the shot could prove impossible.

The three men were passing the alleyway. Frank pressed himself back. It seemed that McAllister's eyes were flicking everywhere. Frank wiped the palms of his hands carefully on the leg of his pants.

McAllister was past now. Frank stayed back where he was for the count of six, unseen and able to see. Then he edged forward, the gun held out of sight. McAllister was turning, facing back Frank's way. The gunman pulled himself back into cover. He found that he had started to sweat. He cursed the deputy. God damn . . .

He peeked out again.

There was a man on the opposite side of the street watching him. Frank ignored him. In a couple of shakes it would all be over.

The prisoner and escort were now almost opposite the saloon. The crowd had thickened. There were several people near Frank, but they were pushing forward toward the saloon. A buggy was stopped by the people in the center of the street. The driver stood up to see better.

Frank started to get desperate.

Call it off, said a voice in his head.

But he wasn't a man easily beaten. The buggy was within a dozen paces of the alleyway. The thought was no sooner in his head, than Frank acted. He ran forward, climbed over the rear of the buggy and instantly had a clear view of his target.

The owner of the buggy turned and bawled out: "What the hell do you reckon you're doin'?"

"I'm doin' no harm, mister," Frank said. "Just gettin' a better look."

"You have the most infernal nerve, sir."

Carson had mounted the sidewalk. McAllister was pushing Evans forward. The target was pretty good. Evans was in view from the waist upward.

Frank sad quietly: "Stay very still, mister, or you get some lead up your butt."

The man froze.

Frank raised the rifle.

McAllister was turning, looking down the street over the heads of the people. Frank sighted on Evans.

McAllister was galvanised into violent action. He seemed to turn and hurl Evans from his feet and throw himself down even as Frank fired.

A man beyond Evans threw up his hands and staggered back.

Frank knew that he had to move fast or it would be his last move. He would have tried for McAllister but the deputy was out of sight. Frank bounded over the side of the buggy and landed flat-footed. A man barred his path, too frightened to move. Frank headed straight for him, throwing him to one side.

A man yelled.

Frank reached the mouth of the alleyway and started down it. He was an active man and he could move fast. He had never moved faster in his life than he did now. He could see Marve in bright sunlight at the end of the dark passage.

It seemed as if he ran down that dark and narrow way forever. The horses were jigging about all over and Marve was having his hands full in holding them.

Marve was moving the animals around so that the black would be handy for Frank to mount. Frank strained to greater effort; his lungs felt as if they would burst. He could hear the air heaving in his chest.

Oh, God, he thought, *I'll never make it before somebody shoots.*

But suddenly the black was right in front of him. He tried to vault into the saddle as he had done so many times before but his legs wouldn't obey him now and he fell heavily against the horse's flank.

Marve was shouting.

Frank got his left foot in the stirrup-iron and heaved himself astride. The loose line was in his hand and the black had taken the jump before he was in the saddle. Marve was spurring away. Without getting his right foot in the iron, Frank hit the black with steel. Marve was already across the vacant lot and was almost to the brush beyond.

Something struck Frank a terrible blow in the back, jarring him forward against the saddlehorn. He grasped the horn with one hand and dropped the rifle. The horse's forward jump that would have become a flat run turned abruptly into a wild pitch. Frank's right hand grasped the coarse mane and he clung on for dear life, hitting the animal with the spurs again, shouting: "Get on, you bastard, get on."

The animal seemed to go crazy at the vicious touch of steel and swerved suddenly. Frank jerked in the saddle as helplessly as a rag-doll, held for a brief moment, then he was hurled loosely from the saddle.

He hit the ground hard on his back and lay there with all the wind knocked out of him.

Marve came pounding back.

"Get on," Frank screamed.

"You hit?"

"I'm a goner. Run for it, you fool. You can't do nothin'."

Feet pounded in the alleyway. A shot winged by. Marve ripped his handgun from leather and fired a couple of shots. His bay was dancing this way and that.

"Run," Frank howled. He tried to raise himself from the ground, but it was as though he were pinned there by a giant stake through his shoulder.

It's caught up with me at last, he thought.

Marve gave him a last desperate look, neck-reined the bay around and went off in a cloud of dust. Booted feet pounded up. Frank tried to draw his gun, but a voice said: "Leave it."

The man reached down, drew the gun and tossed it aside. Frank saw that it was McAllister. He heard the beat of Marve's retreat going away into distance. He should do all right with two fast horses. The law would never catch up with him.

Another man ran up. This was Carson the marshal.

McAllister said: "One down an' one to go."

"Where you hit, Frank?" Carson asked.

"In the back," Frank said. "The only way you could do it, McAllister."

The deputy pursed his lips, but didn't answer.

"I'll get some men to carry him down to the doc's," he said. He walked away down the alleyway.

Carson said: "We'll patch you up, then we'll have a little pow-wow, Frank."

Frank grinned a little.

"You know where'll that'll get you."

"I'm goin' to get you on the end of a rope, Frank, an' you know that."

"But you won't get Marve. He's got two of the fastest horses in Kansas," Frank said. That pleased Frank. He didn't care much what happened to himself now. He was a fatalist. When a man's time came, he went and there wasn't much he could do about it. He waited patiently for the men to come to carry him to the doctor's and wondered idly if he would bleed to death before they got him there. It would save a whole lot of trouble if he did.

6

CARSON heard horses outside on the street. He walked to the door and looked out. McAllister was in the act of dismounting from his canelo. In his hand he held the lead rope of a chunky-looking dun.

Carson said: "Where do you think you're goin'?"

"After Marve Little."

"Are you hell?"

"I am hell."

"I don't remember giving an order."

"That's because you never gave it. I'm doin' you the courtesy of stoppin' by an' tellin' you, ain't I? An' me in a hurry too."

"Just stop to think, Rem. You can't catch Marve. He's an hour ahead and he has real classy horseflesh."

McAllister grinned maddeningly.

"They'll be run belly-deep into the

95

ground while my canelo's still steppin' proud. If Marve knew my horse's kind he'd turn around an' give hisself up."

"All right," Carson said in disgust. "So you have a fancy horse. Maybe the town needs you here."

"Hire yourself another deputy. I'll resign till I hit town again. Use your head, man—Frank dies an' all we have is Evans. We want every man in this outfit we can get. They couldn't kill one prisoner. You think they're goin' to have a chance with two or even three?"

"They could raid the jail while you're gone."

"Fort up and hold out till I get back. This won't take a couple of days."

Carson went red in the face.

"You get in that saddle an' you're fired."

McAllister said: "You almost sound as if you mean that."

"I *do* mean it."

"You're just worried that nasty Marve'll shoot holes in me. You really care, marshal."

Carson became incoherent. McAllister mounted and Carson stamped his feet, yelling: "You're fired."

"I was never fired by a nicer feller."

McAllister turned the canelo toward the creek and set it off down the street at a lope, the dun following briskly behind, Carson swore on for a full minute before he stomped furiously back into his office. The Texas cowhand behind bars said: "What happened, marshal? You look kinda mad."

"You want your teeth knocked in?" Carson demanded.

"No, siree."

"Then don't talk. Don't even breathe loud."

McAllister crossed the creek and turned south, cutting a little west until he struck the sign left by Marve Little. Not long after he lost the sign among the mass of cattle tracks there. He was irritated by this because he knew that it might be hours before he picked up Marve's sign again. But he kept on going. Luck was with him and he saw, when he picked up the sign again, that Marve must be traveling in an almost dead straight line. But Marve had the advantage and McAllister knew it. McAllister would have to stop when it grew dark, because sign couldn't be followed when you couldn't see it. Marve would keep on going. Mile after mile would be eaten up as the man ahead switched from one horse to another. There wasn't much going in McAllister's favor. He wanted some luck.

He rode hard, letting the willing canelo make its own brisk pace. The animal loved to run. The chunky dun, riderless, kept up well. Around noon, McAllister switched the saddle to the back of the dun and tried it out. The man in the livery had sworn the animal was a stayer and McAllister's eyes told him the same thing. As soon as McAllister was up the animal hit a fast long trot and kept it till mid-afternoon when McAllister transferred himself back to the canelo again. By now he was sure that he had a good horse in the dun. His chances of catching Marve were better, but not good. The man had two thoroughbreds with him. McAllister could only hope that they didn't possess the endless bottom that his two horses with their mustang ancestry had.

The flatness of the country started to disappear. It started to roll. It was still possible at times to see a great distance, but there was low land between the ridges that were out of sight. A pursuer could never be too sure that the pursued was not over the next ridge, waiting.

McAllister pressed on hard till dark. He stopped then for two reasons. One, because he couldn't see Marve's tracks any more. Two, because he heard the whinny of a horse. He halted, ground-hitched his two horses, took out the Henry and went cautiously up the next ridge.

Jim Carson was nervous and he had every right to be. He was no coward, but he knew real danger when he saw it. McAllister had shown lack of responsibility and an indifference to danger that angered the marshal. But he knew that his firing of the man was meaningless. He needed McAllister and he had never needed a man more.

So Carson sat at his desk and worried. Frank Little was at the doctor's house wounded. And Carson needed Frank alive. He might die of his wounds, he might be killed in the same way as he had tried to kill Burt Evans.

Evans was another worry. He was in the cell with the Texas cowhand, but how long would he stay there? There was menace in this town and it was doubly worrying because Carson had no idea from whence the menace came. He ran his mind over names again and again, trying to guess at the men who were big enough and dangerous enough to run a business like this. More and more, as he thought, he came to agree with McAllister's hunch that Malloy's killing and the bank robbery were tied in together. He couldn't prove it, but it was a feeling he had.

His main trouble was that he wanted to

be in two places at once. He needed to keep an eye on the jail and he should be with Frank Little.

Mid-morning, the mayor came fussing in. Homer Touch was something of a laugh, but he was no fool. He knew that trouble was brewing and he knew you couldn't fight trouble without the expenditure of money. Money was the mayor's weapon. It could buy guns and it could buy men. He understood at once when Carson put his case to him. Carson glossed over McAllister's departure and said that it was unavoidable and necessary. Touch didn't quite agree with that, but he went along with the marshal.

"Mr. Carson, you need help," he said. "The town isn't made of money, but I daresay it would run to a special deputy. Say, till McAllister gets back. Or things look more settled. We'll consult each day. Hire a man at a rate of fifteen dollars a week. You know a good man?"

"I know a good man. But whether I can get him or not is another matter."

The mayor departed fussily.

Carson stepped onto the sidewalk, spotted a small boy and whistled him. The youngster came running.

"You know Pat O'Doran, son?"

"Sure, marshal."

"Is he in town?"

"Lappin' it up in the Golden Fleece."

Carson flipped a coin and the boy caught it deftly.

"Go fetch him for me."

The kid sped off.

Five minutes later, O'Doran's bulk heaved itself into the office.

"Sit down, Pat."

The giant Irishman punished an inoffensive chair. It groaned.

"You look worried as hell man," he said.

Carson said: "Would you like a rest from railroad work for a few days?"

"I'd be takin' my rest over at the Golden Fleece right this very minute if you hadn't sent for me."

"Can you use a shot-gun?"

Pat laughed.

"I used to shoot a red coat for breakfast

102

every day back in the old country," he said. "You're askin' a whole lot of mighty strange questions, Jim, and I suspect where they're leadin' us."

"Rem and I want help, Pat. An' we want it bad. Would you swear in as a special deputy for a few days."

Pat slapped his massive thigh and roared.

"Pat O'Doran a polisman. I never thought I'd live to see the day . . . my dear old father would turn over in his grave. My sainted mother'd have forty fits, she would."

"Will you do it?"

"Sure, I'll do it. Anythin' to help two old friends out."

Carson swore him in. Evans and the Texas cowhand were interested spectators. The marshal gave his new deputy a badge, a shotgun and a pocketful of shells. The Irishman was as pleased with the weapon as a child with a new toy.

"What do I do first?" he demanded.

"Frank Little is wounded at the doctor's place. I want him down here where I can keep an eye on him." He explained the whole situation to O'Doran. When he finished, Pat said: "By the Holy Mother and all the saints! You need me, Jim boy." He laughed, he looked like he would break into song. "This is better than railroading any day of the week." He agreed that he would go and get Frank Little himself. Sure, carrying the man down here would be no trouble at all.

"You'll need the greener," Carson told him. "Go borrow Altmeyer's buggy. I'll cover you from the other side of the street. I can see the doctor's and this place from there."

The Irishman hurried away, bearing his badge and the shotgun proudly. Carson was pleased. He knew that he had a man there who would never back down. He chose a carbine from the rack and crossed the street to stand near the bank. Penshurst was outside, his hands in his pockets. Carson nodded, but it was as if the banker didn't see him. Carson didn't blame him. He wouldn't be seeing much if he were a ruined man. He watched Pat bring the buggy up to the doctor's house and go inside. The doctor would protest, but he knew that he was holding dynamite while he held Frank. Ten minutes later, Pat came out, holding the tall man easily in his arms. He set him down gently in the bed of the buggy, then he had a good look around. So did Carson. He doubted anything would happen now, but you never knew. He put his thumb into the lever of the carbine, ready to jerk a shell into the breech. Pat was climbing onto the buggy's seat, picking up the shotgun and placing it across his knees. People had stopped to look. Even Penshurst was now paying attention. Pat had the lines in his hands and the horses were on the move, walking up the street. Carson watched the street, running his eyes over the houses, inspecting every watcher in every window. A curtain fluttered. The Darcy brothers were outside the Golden Fleece.

I wonder how much you boys know, Carson thought.

The buggy at last drew up outside the

office. Carson crossed the street and stood around while Pat carried the wounded man into the office. He laid Frank on the pallet bed they had prepared. There was no room in the cell so Frank would have to stay in the office itself.

The gunman looked pale. His dark and fevered eyes watched their every move.

"You could of killed me, movin' me that way," he said.

"Sure," Carson said and covered him with a couple of blankets.

"I reckon you don't have any right to treat a wounded man this way," Frank said.

"I don't want you killed the way you tried to kill Evans," Carson said. "I want you killed in the law's good time."

Evans at the grill said: "What do you mean? He tried to kill me? You're crazy. Frank would never try to kill me. He's a friend. What're you tryin' to pull?"

"I know what they're tryin' to pull, Burt," Frank said. "But it won't do them any good."

"Sure I'm tryin' to pull something,"

Carson said. "I want to scare you into talkin', Evans. An' that's what I'm goin' to do. You're goin' to scare like you never scared before. Because you've got somethin' to be scared of. Marve and Frank was hired to cut you down. McAllister got Frank and Marve got away. He won't get far because McAllister's gone after him."

Frank said: "He don't stand a chance. Marve'll be in Mexico before McAllister reaches the New Mexico line."

"Want to bet on it?"

"Sure."

"Ten dollars says you wrong."

"Done."

Evans said: "It's a lie. Say it's a lie, Frank."

"It's a lie."

Evans had a hold of the bars and he was sweating. His hair was all over his face and his eyes were wild.

"Why would the boss want me dead?" he demanded.

"What boss?" Carson asked.

"He's ravin'," Frank said. "You kicked

a scare into him, Carson. The way he is, he'll say anythin'."

"He's goin' to say plenty by the time I'm through with him," Carson said. "If he don't, you will."

"Me? You should know better."

Pat pled: "Let me work on that Evans a little, Jim. I'll make him sing like a bird."

"No call," said Carson. "He'll sing our tune before the day's out. He'll have to if he wants to save his neck. If he don't he'll hang."

"Hang?" Evans almost screamed. "Hang? You can't hang me. I'm here for carrying a gun and assaulting a peace office. You can't hang a man for that."

Carson walked to the bars.

"I can hang a man for robbery under arms and murder."

"Murder?" Evans frankly screamed this time. "Who said anything about murder?"

"I did."

"Who did I murder?"

"Art Malloy."

There was a short and stunned silence.

108

Evans said: "I didn't kill Malloy. Why should I want to kill Malloy? I didn't have a reason even."

"Your orders were your reason."

"What orders? I never took orders from anybody."

Carson said: "I don't want to discuss it with you, Evans. You stay in there and sweat and you think. Think what it'll be like when you feel the rope around your neck."

Frank was grinning.

"You got him scared all right, Carson," he said.

Carson walked across the office and looked down at the wounded man.

"You don't have too much to grin about, Frank," he said. "You're in the same position. It's risky having you alive now. And you failed to kill Evans."

"Who said I was tryin' to kill Evans?"

"You mean you have the nerve to deny it?"

"I was tryin' to kill you an' McAllister and you know it."

From the cell, Evans shouted: "I heard

that. He wasn't trying to kill me. He was trying to kill you and McAllister. He just made a liar out of you, Carson."

The marshal threw up his hands.

"Believe what you want," he said. 'It's all the same to me. Let's have a drink, Pat."

He found a bottle. He poured for Pat and himself. They drank. Frank Little closed his eyes and slept. He didn't seem to have a care in the world. Evans went and lay on his bed. The Texas cowhand built cigarettes and smoked them endlessly. He coughed occasionally. The day dragged on. Finally, Carson said: "We should try an' get some sleep. Maybe we won't get any tonight."

He got some blankets and made up a rough bed behind the desk. Pat knew that he didn't mean to leave the office till he had the prisoners off his hands. Pat didn't want to sleep—he was a man who needed little. So Carson lay down and was soon off, while Pat sat outside on a chair, tilted back, shotgun in hand and pipe in mouth. People glanced at him curiously as they passed. He smiled and nodded to them pleasantly.

Tonight, he thought, would be the time. If something was going to be done it would be done under cover of darkness. He had a feeling that he was going to earn his money.

7

AROUND the start of darkness that day, two significant things happened to help the drama on its way.

One, McAllister crept up the nearest ridge and spotted a horse grazing placidly on the buffalo grass. It was a fine thoroughbred black and McAllister reckoned it could belong only to Frank Little.

It could be the bait of a trap, of course. But he thought not, unless the horse was sound. Then it was a trap. But he wasn't going to inspect the horse till he was sure there was no trap. With the Henry held at the ready, he circled the spot, keeping under cover of the ridges, not hurrying, knowing that hurry had killed many a good man.

It was the best part of an hour before he was pretty sure that there was no trap.

He approached the black. The animal lifted its head and watched him. As soon as he got near, the black sidestepped and tried to run. The trailing rein made him stumble. McAllister pounced on the line and held it. At once, the animal stood. McAllister looked it over. It was saddled and bridled and, though it had been run hard, looked in good condition. He lifted the forefeet one at a time and inspected them. Nothing was amiss. But when he inspected the off hind foot, he found the loose shoe. So Marve had left the horse because of a loose shoe. McAllister let the foot drop.

He stood and thought awhile.

Marve now had one horse. He might ride on all night. He might rest and save his horse. If he knew what he was at, he would rest. McAllister might catch him tomorrow.

He went back and fetched his own two horses and brought them to the black. The canelo didn't like the look of the black and went for it. McAllister staked them far apart. There wasn't much wood around, but he managed to build a small fire and by its light, he worked on the black's shoe. By the time he finished, he reckoned it would last a day or two. Then he thought some more. If Marve couldn't find time to repair the shoe, he must be in an almighty hurry. In such a hurry that he most likely hadn't stopped to rest the night. On thinking further, McAllister reckoned that the shoe had come loose with a couple of hours of daylight to go. That then could have been the reason for Marve pushing on. He wanted to get as far as he could go in daylight. Tomorrow might see him caught after all.

The following day, McAllister was in the saddle by first light. He had three horses now and he ran harder than ever. The pace might be hard on the man, but the three fine horses took little heed of it. The black, he had to admit, was every bit as much horse as the canelo was so far as speed was concerned, but he doubted it had the staying power. He reckoned if he didn't run Marve down that day, he didn't know horses.

He rode right through the day without a stop, never pausing at noon, except to switch the saddle from the canelo to the dun. An hour later, he switched to the black and stepped the pace up a mite. The big horse liked to run and he surely ran it. Then, late in the afternoon, he spotted the lone figure ahead of him. He knew then unless darkness saved Marve, he would have him.

The other significant thing that happened that first night was that Drummond went to see Fred Darcy. That in itself was significant. It had never happened before.

He found the two Darcys in their office drinking whiskey. They were startled at the sight of him.

"What happened?" Fred demanded, jumping to his feet.

Drummond said coldly: "You ask what happened when Evans is down at the jail with Frank Little alongside him? If one of them talks we could all hang."

Johnny went pale.

"Is that right, Frank tried to kill McAllister?"

"And Evans," Drummond told him. "Evans is our weak link. They can tear Frank to pieces, but he'll never talk."

Fred said: "I ain't met the man who won't talk soon or late."

"Well, they're got to be stopped," Drummond said. They looked at him. They had never seen their cool chief so disturbed. It rattled them to see him so. "We've either got to get them out of there or kill them. I don't mind much which."

"Have you got the men to do it?" Fred wanted to know.

"I've got men." He walked to the table and poured himself a whiskey. He drank it off before he resumed. "Fred, I need somebody smart to lead them."

Fred Darcy twisted his full face in a wry grin.

"That means me."

"That means you."

"That means bracing McAllister." Fred didn't hide the fact that he didn't like that.

116

"He's out of town and liable to stay out for some time. He's after Marve and Marve had two very good horses with him. He'll take some catching. What I want done I want done tonight."

"Tonight?" Fred looked a mite startled.

"If Evans hasn't cracked already, he soon will. We have to stop him quickly."

Johnny said eagerly: "Don't you give it another thought, Drummond. Me and Fred'll stop him."

Fred growled: "You stay out of this."

"Like hell I do."

"Now you listen to me, Johnny . . ."

Drummond said: "Let him go along, Fred. He's good with a gun."

Fred had been protecting his wild younger brother for years. It was said that he had saved him from hanging on more than one occasion.

They sat at the table and drank some more whiskey. Drummond talked. He explained the set-up down at the jail. The marshal and one deputy were the only guards. Two men only needed two bullets. Who was the deputy now McAllister was out of town? Pat O'Doran. That made the brothers laugh. One simple fighting Irishman. They'd settle his hash. This would give Johnny an added incentive because once O'Doran had boxed his ears as if he were a kid. They must make their raid in the early hours; surprise must be on their side. They must be ruthless and quick. If they could get Frank out of there alive, they were to do so. If not, they were to kill him. Fred demanded to know what they would get out of it. Drummond showed some anger. What did they expect? If Evans or Frank talked, they'd hang. Wasn't that enough incentive. They argued. Drummond relented and named a sum. It wasn't as much as the Darcys wanted. They reached a compromise which was the sum Drumond had first thought of. He departed and left two shaken men behind him. When he reached the backlots, he smiled to himself with satisfaction. It had seemed a short while ago that things were starting to go against him. He didn't like that. Now he saw that even in a temporary defeat he could derive some profit. He would have the Darcys on the run tomorrow. He would take over the goldmine of the Golden Fleece at a knockdown price.

He crossed the backlot, smiling. The bank was as good as his. He had put that pompous fool Penshurst on his feet again, but it was him who was propping the man up. The daughter was falling like ripe fruit into his hands. He would make his stake here, then he would return to the East where he could live a cultured and respectable life. Emily would like that. She was just what he wanted. She would be dependent on him, but she would be a beautiful decoration to his life. Other men would envy him for her; she would fit into any society. Yes, he was on the way.

He let himself in the kitchen of his house and his housekeeper looked up from her sewing.

"How did it go?"

"The Darcys'll do it."

"Let's hope they make a real job of it this time and don't bungle it like those Littles did."

"You should have been born a man, Clarissa," Drummond said.

"I'm a better man than you'll ever be," she snapped. He hurried from the room, wondering why he didn't cut adrift from the woman.

Emily Penshurst sat reading a book. Her father stood at the window of the house he could no longer afford and looked over Garrett. He wondered how his daughter could so cut herself off from what he regarded as his personal tragedy. She went about her life calmly, almost gaily, as if nothing had happened. He turned his head to watch her.

She reminded him of her mother, dead these ten yeas. Sarah had been a clear-headed woman, always the driving force in the family. But he hadn't done so badly on his own. He had built up a tight little bank here, he had been respected and liked. He wondered if he would ever be able to climb back. It was his own esteem he wanted to reach again. Now he was nothing more than Will Drummond's clerk.

He thought about Drummond. That man's manner had changed toward him in the last few days. Some of the politeness had gone. His attentions to Emily had become more obvious. At times it had been downright embarrassing. But he, Penshurst, had not dared to say anything. He knew why. It was not because he was now in Drummond's power, but because he wanted to see the girl married to the man. He wanted Emily's future to be secure.

How much did he trust Drummond? With money; with his daughter. Unease stirred in Penshurst. He did not know on which count.

He turned.

"I think we should talk, daughter," he said. He tried to make his voice gentle, but he could hear the strain in it.

At once, she looked up, smiling.

"Of course," she said. "Talk by all means, papa."

"About you."

"Me?" She sounded faintly surprised.

"You and Will."

"Oh, papa, do we have to?" She looked modestly flustered, but Penshurst wasn't taken in for a moment. Emily had been adept at being modestly flustered from the age of ten.

"How serious is it between you two?" he demanded.

"Do we have to be so blunt?" She looked just the slightest bit cross. She did it very prettily.

"Yes, I'm afraid we do," he said. "The situation is—ah—calls for bluntness. Frankly, the sooner I see you settled the better. Has Will said anything to lead you to believe . . ."

"Do you mean has he proposed, papa?"

"That's what I mean."

"Not in so many words."

"But he has hinted?"

"Well," she cast down her eyes and blushed, "he's very ardent. Nobody could

122

complain about Will's ardor. He's attentive. If he didn't mean to propose to me one day, his behavior is peculiar to say the least."

"This is no time for joking, miss."

"I'm not joking. Indeed, I take the matter seriously. My future is at stake after all."

"Emily," he said, "he must ask you soon. Very soon. I cannot provide for you in the way you have been accustomed. I am penniless now. We must face that fact. I want you settled, child, then I can rest easy." He waited, watching her face. She did not look up at him. At last he said: "May I enquire your feelings for him?"

She looked at him now, surprised.

"Why, I have him in the highest regard."

"Do you love him?"

For a moment, he penetrated through the armor of her performance. She looked at him, her lips slightly parted and he saw objectively how beautiful a woman she was. She seemed dismayed at his question.

"Do I have to answer that, father?"

"No, my child, not if it distresses you," he told her. "But selfish as I may be, I would not wish you married to a man you couldn't love."

"I've put love away," she said in a voice so low he could scarcely hear her.

"Why?" he asked gently.

"I'd rather not say."

He looked out onto the street again, not seeing the traffic in the lamplight.

"Was it the marshal?" he asked.

"Yes," she said simply.

"I'd rather thought so," he told her. He turned and put a hand on her shoulder. For a moment there was real tenderness between father and daughter, an emotion that had not been expressed between them for a long time. She reached up and laid her hand on his.

"I don't want you to marry Will for me," he said. "We'll manage without that if you wish. It's just that I want to know you'll be settled in the future."

"I know," she assured him.

"Promise you won't do anything against your own wishes for my sake."

"I promise. But don't worry about me, papa. Something in me died when Art Malloy died. Feelings don't matter too much to me any more."

"Is there something about Will that worries you?" he asked.

"Nothing."

"Are you telling me the truth?"

"Yes, papa."

And he had to be satisfied with that.

McAllister couldn't see the figure ahead of him clearly because the distance was so great, but he didn't doubt that it was Marve Little. No sooner did he sight him than he swung to the west into the cover of the nearest ridge, angled south-west for a while and then angled south-east relying on his superior speed to carry out the plan he had in mind. It was simple enough: get ahead or alongside his quarry and start from there.

He was mounted on the black now, the horse was fast and he urged it on to its utmost with voice, spur and quirt, not hurting it, but demanding its best. The big horse responded nobly as he knew it would. They ran for something like three miles, topped a ridge and sighted their quarry slightly to their rear, running along the next ridge. McAllister at once dropped his lead lines and left the canelo and dun to their own devices, relying on the canelo's good sense and the dropped lines to hold them. He now swung east and headed to cut Marve off.

Swinging down from the ridge, he hit the flat and the big black extended itself, crossed the flat in record time and strained up the ridge in front of it.

As soon as they topped the rise, Marve sighted them and pulled his horse to a halt. The distance between the two men was about two hundred yards. One glance even at that distance was enough to tell McAllister that Marve's horse was bushed. There was a limit to what even a good horse could do.

McAllister turned straight toward Marve and sent the black along the rounded and wide crest of the ridge, wanting to get as close as he could before the shooting, if any, started. Marve at once swung down from his horse, ripped his rifle from the boot and took cover behind the animal, resting the rifle-barrel across the saddle.

McAllister wasn't crazy. Unless he had to, he wasn't charging down that rifle barrel. If he did, he or the black were dead. He pulled the now heaving animal to a halt, slid from the saddle and pulled out the Henry. He moved away from the black because he didn't want the animal hit. He jacked a shell into the breech and he and Marve stared at each other for a moment.

"I'm takin' you back, Marve," he called.

"Frank . . ." Marve shouted back. "How about Frank? Did you kill him?"

"Frank's alive," McAllister shouted back. "And maybe talkin' by now."

"Not Frank," Marve replied. "Come an' get me, McAllister."

Like hell I do, McAllister thought. All

he could see of the man was his head and shoulders and the lower part of his legs. Not much of a target.

He raised his rifle and snapped off a shot, knowing that he was shooting high for fear of killing the horse. He hated to kill a horse. He knew he was a damned fool, but he couldn't do anything about it. His old man had been the same way. He fired but he moved as he did so, throwing himself to one side and down the slope of the ridge. He rolled, hit brush and heard two shots come from Marve. They didn't come too near, for which he was duly thankful.

He looked around. The land was pretty broken here. It was a damp bottom with a glisten of water showing through the brush to his right. Here and there were a few stunted trees. He wished he had stayed nearer the black. Marve could get away, with him down here on foot. Also he might try to reach the black which was a mite fresher than his own animal. McAllister could see the black standing motionless above him, line dangling. Marve was now out of sight.

McAllister got to his feet and, crouched up, ran forward a dozen or so yards, flung himself down behind some brush and waited for a minute. He heard nothing. Getting to his feet again, he started slowly and cautiously up the ridge.

He heard the sound of a man running.

Heaving himself up and forward, McAllister charged to the top of the ridge and came out on its rounded shoulder. He spotted Marve at once, legging it toward the black.

McAllister halted and placed the butt of the Henry in his right shoulder.

"Hold it, Marve."

The man ran on. As he came near the black, the horse pranced away from him. He grabbed for the line and missed. The black ran a few yards off, trumpeting. McAllister could hear Marve's shout of rage.

"Come on back, Marve," McAllister called.

The man's reply was to pull his belt-gun from its holster, raise it for a careful aim and fire. It was a long shot for a pistol, but Marve didn't miss by more than inches. McAllister swore. He fired.

It was as if a giant hand had plucked Marve's right leg from under him. He toppled over and fell on his face. McAllister levered a fresh shot into his rifle. Marve heaved himself up on one elbow and fired a shot. It went wide.

McAllister shouted: "Throw it down or I'll kill you."

Marve hesitated for a moment, then he tossed the gun wide. McAllister walked to the bay, not taking his eyes from the fallen man, and picked up the trailing line. He led the horse to Marve and looked down at him.

"You damn fool," McAllister said. "No call for you to get shot."

The stream of abuse that came from Marve indicated that McAllister's family had not had a birth certificate for a long time. Several generations, in fact.

"Any hidden guns, knives or anything else?" McAllister asked. Marve shook his head and sat up. He was holding his right calf and looking pretty green around the gills.

"I'll bleed to death," he said.

McAllister told him: "Take your boot off and roll your pants up." The man obeyed, his face twisted in shock and pain. McAllister leaned on his rifle, bending down and inspecting the wound. He had sent the bullet through the fleshy part of the leg. It had entered the front and gone out of the back. He said: "You'll live. But I don't see why you should."

Marve twisted and kicked him in the face with his left foot. McAllister turned a somersault and dropped his rifle. He lay there for a second, feeling as if the whole of his face had been smashed in. Marve moved as quickly as his wounded leg would allow and dove for the discarded belt-gun. He got a hand on it and McAllister came uncertainly to his feet, jumping into the air and landing on Marve's back with both feet. It knocked the wind out of the man, but it didn't stop him rolling and throwing McAllister clear. Nor did it stop him coming up with the gun in his hand, cocked. McAllister came to his hands and knees and stared into the dark and lethal eye of the gun.

It was surrender or move and McAllister was moving before the thought of surrender entered his head. He hurled himself to the right as the gun boomed. The lead plucked at his sleeve, then he was throwing himself at the man in front of him. Hastily, Marve fired again, but that did not stop McAllister's fist from crashing into his face. Marve went backward and hit with his shoulder. McAllister dropped both knees into the man's belly and the wind went out of him noisily. Marve made one more feeble effort and McAllister hit him in the face again.

Marve lay still.

His face was ruined, which, McAllister thought, was plain justice after all. His own face felt as if it was ruined for ever.

He took the fallen man's gun and shoved it under his belt. Then he staggered to the black, took down the canteen from the saddlehorn and took a drink. He washed his face in the tepid water and felt a little better. His legs felt as if they were made of rubber. He took a peggin string from a pocket and bound Marve's hands behind his back.

Then he tore up a shirt in his saddle-pocket and made a pad and bandage for the wound in the man's leg. Marve woke up while that was going on. He tried to kick McAllister who said: "Lie quiet or I'll bend a gun-barrel over your fool head." After that he lay quiet. McAllister dragged him to his feet and heaved him into the black's saddle. He sat there, hunched up and in pain.

"It'll kill me to ride," he protested.

"Too bad," said McAllister. He mounted the other horse and led the way back to his own horses. He found them grazing peacefully. The canelo was glad to see him. He heaved Marve out of the saddle and left him lying on his back while he put Marve's saddle on the dun and his own on the canelo. After that, he was ready for the ride.

He wondered how Jim Carson was making out in town.

8

IT was a puzzle to Fred Darcy to know how to get into the marshal's office and carry out Will Drummond's design. He had no doubt that the bar would be on the door. The windows, he knew, were not barred, but the wooden shutters might be closed. If the windows were not shuttered, then he could get his work done all right. A burning torch thrown into the center of the office would light the place up and the shooting could be done through the windows. If the windows were shuttered, he would have to talk himself in at the door, but that meant giving away his identity.

So he was worried. His younger brother Johnny thought the whole thing was a lark. Which was Johnny all over. He could never see further than the end of his nose. But he was a handy man to take on a trip like this and no mistake.

He was a sure shot and he had plenty of nerve.

The men gathered in the creekside shack. There were six of them beside the Darcy brothers. Fred knew all of them there and he didn't like the look of any of them much. It was the viciousness and violence that showed in their faces that put him off, for there was too much of both in his own nature for him to shy from them. It was the fact that he knew them and realised that they were not in his class. These were men who liked jobs that went their way all the time. They were hard enough when it came to shooting other men, but they would not welcome lead singing about their own ears. If it came to the push, it would be just him and Johnny. Even as he spoke to them, he wondered if it wouldn't be better for him and his brother to do the job on their own. But Drummond had willed that they take part in the raid and Darcy, often against his own nature, found himself falling in with Drummond's wishes.

When they were ready and assembled, he gave them their instructions. He gave them simply and firmly. If they did their job right, they'd be paid. If they pulled out at a crucial moment, the Darcys would kill them. Fred didn't mince matters. This was the kind of talk these men understood. They nodded. Fred wished he had Frank and Marve Little here. They were better than this trash. He smiled ironically to himself. It was Frank they were maybe going to kill. That was the way life went.

"Lead off in twos," he said, "an' keep it quiet. Move in when you see me make the first move. It'll be like either way I described to you."

They moved off in twos, none of them wearing spurs, all of them with loaded guns in their holsters. Soon only the two brothers were left.

Fred looked at his hunter and saw it was four o'clock.

"How'd you feel?" he asked.

"Just fine," the younger man replied.

"I'd be even better if we didn't have that bunch along."

Fred said: "I was thinking the same thing."

They left the shack and walked through the brush that grew along the creek side. They angled right, went through timber and reached the backlots of the town. It was very dark and they had to walk with caution.

Fred halted and Johnny walked into him.

"This is it," Fred said. "Got the torch?"

"Sure."

For a second, both men were tensely silent, listening to the beats of their own hearts. Fred led the way forward silently, going along the side of the office and out onto the sidewalk. They walked on tiptoe. Fred paused for a moment, scanning the street, looking for any citizen who might be about, checking if any of the other men were showing themselves. Nothing moved.

Johnny felt in his pocket for a lucifer, found one and brought it out.

Fred went forward and at once saw a light burning low in the office. So the windows weren't shuttered. For the sake of coolness, the marshal had failed to take that precaution. Fred ran his eyes over the scene in front of him. He could not see much except a man lying on a cot to the right and a couple of forms laid out on the floor.

He lifted his Colt's gun from leather and whispered: "Strike a light."

Johnny ran the lucifer over his butt and it failed to light.

He said: "Godammit," softly like a prayer. He tried again. The match flared. He seemed to hesitate.

Fred's nerves were raw. He expected a shot at any moment.

"Get on," he whispered urgently.

Johnny put the match to the torch and it flared at once. Fred went into action, striking at the glass of the window with the barrel of his gun again and again so that a gaping hole appeared. As soon as it was large enough, Johnny hurled the torch into the center of the office.

At once the waking startled men came into stark view.

A man stumbled from the floor, throwing aside a blanket. Fred fired at him. He made a big target and Fred couldn't miss at that range. The man was hurled back against the desk, dropping the shot-gun he held in one hand. Johnny drew his gun and, crouched down below the window, started firing into the room. Feet pounded across the street as the other men came up. Fred dropped down by Johnny and caught sight of a man in the cell at the far end of the office. Fred thought he could hear him scream. He pumped three shots at him.

There was a man behind the desk, shooting. Johnny turned his gun on him.

The man on the cot rolled onto the floor and stretched out for the fallen shotgun. Fred fired at him and found that his gun was empty.

The other men had reached the window to the right and were smashing the glass in, firing into the horror of the office. The man behind the desk slid from sight. Fred got down against the wall of the office and hastily tumbled fresh shells into the gun. The noise was deafening and when he shouted to his brother, the words were as nothing.

The man on the floor lifted the shotgun, lined it up with a shadowy figure at the window and let fly with both barrels. Some of the lead that was smashing the office to pieces struck him. He dropped the shotgun and lay down. Now Frank Little was dying.

The blast from the shotgun lifted Johnny Darcy and drove him back onto the street. He fell in a boneless heap and lay moaning. Fred shoved his gun away into leather and leapt down from the sidewalk, falling on one knee beside his brother.

"Johnny . . . Johnny . . ."

The other men were running like frightened dogs.

"Stop," Fred cried out. "Help me with him."

They ran on.

There was a silence that was awesome after the deafening racket. Fred looked around desperately. A man was running down the street toward him. Somebody in the marshal's office was calling feebly for help.

For a moment, Fred panicked.

He heaved his gun from the leather and fired two shots at the approaching man. The fellow veered to one side, appeared to trip on his feet and went down. There was movement further down the street.

He must get Johnny home. He must get him home and get a doctor to him. He could think of nothing else. He put his gun away and lifted his brother from the ground and started walking. He walked across the street and down the alleyway that ran alongside the bank. In his head a voice told him that you could do a thing like that at a time like this and get away with it if the luck was with you. There were shouts from the street and the sound of men running. He turned right and walked along the rear of the houses, stumbling on the trash, feeling Johnny's full weight now. He was a powerful man physically, but he was tiring rapidly. As he walked, he talked to Johnny, begging him to say something and show him that he was still alive.

It was years since he had prayed, but now he whispered: *Please God let him live.*

At last he came to the rear of the Golden Fleece and laid Johnny down on the edge of the loading platform. He knew the rear door would be locked. Bolted on the inside. Bob Brody, his man, would either be asleep or out front finding out about the shooting. God knew it had been loud enough to wake the dead. He threw his weight against the door. It cracked loudly. He backed and hurled himself against it again. This time it flew open.

He hurried inside, groped his way down the long passage and found the door to the office. In there he lit a lamp, then half-ran back to Johnny. He carried his brother into the office and lay him on the couch there.

The young man was an appalling sight. He had taken both blasts of the shotgun. Half his face seemed to have been taken away and his chest was torn open in places to the bone. But there was so much blood that Fred couldn't assess the full damage.

"My God," he said and stood helplessly for the moment, not knowing where to start.

The doctor! He must have the doctor.

He turned to the door. The thought struck him that Johnny might bleed to death while he was fetching the man. Johnny groaned.

"Fred."

He turned back to his brother, falling on his knees beside him.

"Hold on, kid," he said, "I'll fix you good."

The boy's eyes were open, staring at Fred in a kind of fixed horror.

"I'm finished."

"You're talking crazy."

144

Fred was on his feet, rushing from the room to the kitchen where he found towels and hot water. He hurried back into the office, dropped a towel in the water and started to wipe the blood from Johnny's face. As fast as he wiped it away, more came in its place. He grew desperate. More blood was seeping steadily from the boy's torso.

"Christ Almighty," he said out loud, "what do I do?"

He was panicking. For Johnny's sake he had to stay calm.

Johnny was trying to sit up, a fixed look on his ghastly face.

"Fred . . ."

The sound was a faint, breathless scream.

Fred caught his brother by the hand. For a second, Johnny's grip was like a vice. Suddenly, it relaxed. Johnny fell back against the couch and a high whine of sound came bubbling from his lips.

"Johnny . . ."

He knew that his brother was dead.

He did not know how long he stayed

there by the couch on one knee, staring wordlessly at his brother's face. His mind flicked back over the past, their early years together, the way he had always protected Johnny, saved him from the results of his scrapes. Protecting Johnny had become a part of life.

Suddenly, he felt a cramping in his limbs. He stood up and found that he was stiff and cold. He started to shake. Death had never affected him before. He had seen men die before and had killed some of them. Now the full import of death came home to him.

He turned and walked to the table. The bottle and two glasses still stood there. Johnny had drunk from one of the glasses not an hour before. An hour ago he had been alive, excited at the prospect of one of his larks. Fred poured himself a stiff drink and tossed it off. He felt a little better, so he took another.

He stood thinking.

Who had killed Johnny?

He thought back over the scene of carnage in the marshal's office, tried to thread his way through that violent deadly minute of time in which men had died. He remembered the big man going down ... the man on the cot had thrown himself on the floor and picked up the shotgun. Fred screwed up his eyes, thinking, straining his mind.

Suddenly, he opened his eyes.

That man had been Frank Little.

The bitter irony of it came home to him. Johnny could have been the man to kill Frank, the man who had killed him. They would never have managed to break into the office. Frank would have to have been killed.

Had he been killed?

Fred looked across at his brother. The sight of him lying there torn and bloody was horribly obscene. Fred walked up the stairs with the lamp in his hand, fetched a blanket from Johnny's room, returned with it and covered his brother. Something eased in his mind, now the boy was out of sight. He gave himself another drink. His hands were still shaking and he could not rid himself of the cold that seemed to penetrate to his very bones. He took out his gun, cleaned it and reloaded.He put on a jacket, turned the lamp low and went out of the front door of the saloon.

Outside on the street, the town seemed as busy as daytime. He looked down the street and saw a great gathering of people around the marshal's office. The buzz of their talk reached him. He went toward them.

One or two men turned to look at him. It dawned on him in a dreamlike way that they had no idea that he had tken part in the shooting. But now they were staring as he came into the brightness of the lamplight, nudging and pointing. He shouldered his way through them, came to the door of the office and found the place full of more men. The air was filled with the stench of cordite; the place was bright with the light of several lamps. The young doctor was busy in the corner bent over a man on the floor. Fred went and looked over his shoulder and saw that the man was Jim Carson, the marshal. It looked like he had been hit in the head and the upper part of the body. His eyes were closed.

Fred turned. A big man was sitting on the floor with his back against the wall. Pat O'Doran. His deputy's badge glittered on his chest. It was buckled where it had been hit by a bullet. Some bloody rag adorned the man's head. More was bound around one hand. He looked like a man deep in shock. How the two men had been able to live through the storm of lead was a puzzle to the Texan. He turned across the room to find a still form lying under a blanket. Bending he lifted back a corner and stared down into Frank Little's face. All the tough bitterness seemed to have been erased from it. It was battered and calm in the lamplight, untouched.

Disappointment touched Fred. He could not now kill the man who had killed Johnny. But at least Frank was dead and that was a reason for some satisfaction.

He replaced the corner of the blanket and looked up. The grilled door of the cell was open. Inside, one man lay on the floor and another on a cot. There were two men attending to the one on the cot. Fred stepped inside. The man on the cot, he didn't know. He was alive and they had put a bandage around the upper part of his left arm. Fred looked at the man on the floor. Burt Evans. One leg drawn up, an arm twisted grotesquely under him, his face contorted with pain and fear. He was dead.

Fred Darcy's mind started to come out of its frozen state and to function. So far so good. The two witnesses were dead. One of the men bent over the cot turned his head and saw him.

"Hello, Fred. My God, look at you."

Fred looked down at himself and saw that the whole of the front of his clothing was soaked with blood. Johnny's blood. For a moment, he was speechless. This could put a rope around his neck, he knew.

He said: "I lifted one of 'em. What a night. I never saw so much blood."

"Butchery," the man said. "This was the work of madmen."

"Sure," Fred said, "only madmen could do a thing like this."

He turned back into the office and almost walked into Touch, the mayor. The man was wringing his hands. What would the outside world think of this? The town's name had been good while Malloy had been alive. Fred patted him sympathetically on the shoulder and went on. He stumbled out onto the street and walked through the crowd. He never remembered going back to his own place, for he was trying to think clearly. He stood for a moment in the vast emptiness of the bar. He was steadier now. Seeing Frank Little dead there had somehow steadied him. He heard a movement behind him and, turning, saw a man silhouetted against the light of the street. His right hand flashed down to his gun. The sound of it cocking was clear in the stillness of the room.

"Who's this?" he demanded.

"Drummond."

"You nearly got yourself killed."

The man came forward.

"Here's the most Godawful mess," Drummond said.

"Evans and Little're dead," Fred said.

"I know. Were any of you seen?"

"I don't think so. Come through into the office." Fred uncocked the gun and put it away, leading the way through the darkness down the passageway and into the office. Drummond stopped in the doorway, staring at the blanket-shrouded figure on the couch.

"Who's that?" he demanded.

Fred poured himself a drink and said: "Take a look."

Drummond stepped forward and lifted back a corner of the blanket. He exclaimed in horror when he saw Johnny's ruined face.

"God in heaven!"

He turned wild eyes on Darcy who looked at him woodenly.

"Frank did it before we got him."

"I'm sorry, Fred," Drummond said. "I can't say how sorry."

"A risk we all took," Fred said. "The kid's luck was against him."

For the first time, Drummond saw the blood on Fred's clothes.

"Look at you, man. You're all covered in blood. Change your clothes and burn those before somebody sees you."

"The whole town's seen me."

"What?"

"I went down there and had a look around."

"You must have been out of your mind."

"I explained it away. Said I'd toted one of their wounded."

But Drummond was shaken.

"You're suspect as it is. You shouldn't have taken the risk. You could get us all in trouble."

Fred said: "I put off suspicion by goin' down there."

"If you went down there, you must know the full score."

"Evans and Frank dead. Carson looks damn nigh dead. O'Doran wounded."

"And are you sure neither of them sighted you?"

"I can't be sure of anythin', can I? It was a risk we took."

Drummond said: "Clean yourself up, man. I must get down there and show myself the responsible citizen I am. Again, I can't say how sorry I am about Johnny. I wouldn't have had it happen for all the world."

"Sure," Fred said.

"I'll get in touch later."

"Sure."

Drummond left. Fred stood hating him.

9

DRUMMOND knew that he would not sleep that night. His mind was in a ferment. This was out of character and disturbed him. He stood at the window of his bedroom watching the shadowy figures of the folks going home from the marshal's office. He could hear the low murmur of their voices. Occasionally, a shout broke the quietness. Clarissa, his housekeeper, was asleep in the next room. Nothing would keep her from her sleep. Nothing worried her. She was the only human being he had ever known who couldn't be shaken by anything.

He had wanted Evans and Little dead. Once they were dead all his problems would be solved. But now they were dead other problems had appeared. Did nothing ever go smoothly. When had things started to go wrong with him? The answer to that was simple—the day McAllister pinned on that badge.

What, he asked himself, was so special about the man? Surely, he was nothing more than the usual Texas cowhand that came up the trail, something between a man and a horse. Then he remembered the stories he had heard about the man: how he was the son of the legendary Chad McAllister. That could mean something. Breeding could tell. The underlying viciousness of the man's character came to the surface—men had died who had stood in his way. McAllister could die too. He was no immortal. Drummond had made one try for him. The next would not fail. But who had he left now for such work except for Fred Darcy. And if Darcy did an open shooting he would have to leave town in a hurry.

Leave town in a hurry . . .

Drummond's mind dwelled on that thought.

Darcy had put them all in jeopardy going down to the marshal's office as he had done with his clothes covered in blood. Already somebody might be suspicious. Maybe Darcy would be better out of town. But he had holdings in the town and would be hard to persuade to go. If Drummond could arrange for Darcy to kill McAllister and then run, Darcy would be under suspicion at once whether he did the killing secretly or not. And if he ran, who would own the Golden Fleece?

There was only one answer to that. Drummond.

The man's cupidity over-reached his caution. He started to plan. He could make Darcy run now and get the best witness against Drummond out of town or he could get him to run after killing McAllister. If he did the latter, Drummond might lose the saloon. It was quite a good idea to make Darcy panic now. He reckoned he could do it. The man was upset after the death of his brother. He was shaken to the core.

What of the men who had helped in the raid on the office? Let them stay quietly in the shack by the creek for a few days and then drift out of the country in ones and twos. They could be a source of danger.

He wondered how long McAllister would be out of town. He was pretty confident that he would not catch Marve. There was no horseflesh in the country like that of the Littles. Marve was safely on his way to Mexico by now and there wouldn't be much money waiting at El Paso for him. But he wouldn't come back in a hurry to talk.

His affairs weren't as tidy as he would have liked, but he wasn't doing too badly, Drummond thought. He had his town property, the bank was as good as his and shortly the gold mine of the saloon would be in his hands. Yes, he would panic Fred tomorrow. He smiled to himself, pleased.

Dawn came with him still at his window, thinking. He heard Clarissa moving about and soon he smelled the delicious aroma of ham and eggs frying. He realised how hungry he was. He shaved and went down into the kitchen.

He sat at the table and Clarissa put a cup of coffee in front of him.

"How did it go?" she asked.

He told her what had happened. He told her also of his thoughts in the dawn hours. She put ham and eggs in front of him and he started to eat; she sat opposite him and sipped coffee.

"Get rid of Darcy," she said. "Get the saloon while you can. This is going to be a boom year for cattle. Maybe next year will be too late. The railhead is moving west. Make money while you can. This may be worthless soon. You'll make more than you do from the rest of your property in town."

"You could be right."

"Have you ever known me wrong."

"Can't say I have."

"Go to Darcy and say that he's suspected. Frighten him."

"He doesn't frighten too easily."

"Any man frightens when he knows he's going to hang."

After breakfast, he changed his clothes and walked down town. There was still a few of the curious around the Marshal's office door. Inside he found that the dead had been removed and the sight of them made him think of Johnny and to wonder what Fred would do with the body. There were several people in the office, most of them women and among them, he was astonished to see Emily Penshurst.

"Whatever are you doing here, Emily?" he enquired.

"Doing what I can to help," she told him. "Oh, Will, did you ever hear of a more dreadful thing? To kill two helpless men and to shoot down the marshal and his deputy . . ."

"Terrible," he said. "It doesn't bear thinking on. But you shouldn't be here, my dear. This isn't at all the place for you."

She smiled at him.

"I'm not made of Dresden china, you know."

He went up to the marshal who was now lying on the cot which Frank Little had occupied. The man's eyes were open, but he still looked dazed.

"Where'd they get you, Jim?" he asked.

"I bounced one off my head," Carson replied hoarsely. "I have the other lodged in my ribs."

"As soon as the doctor allows you to be moved," Drummond said, "I'll have you brought up to my house. You'll be taken good care of there."

"Thanks, Drummond," the marshal said. "I wouldn't want to be a nuisance."

"The least I can do."

As he turned away, Emily came up to him.

"That was really nice of you, Will," she said.

"A man feels so helpless, so little he can do. We can't undo what's done, we can only try to help a little." She patted his arm. "You're looking tired, my dear. Maybe you should go home and try to rest."

"Soon."

They exchanged smiles and, as Drummond turned to leave, he found himself faced by the mayor.

Touch was a little distraught.

"To think this could happen in our town, Will," he cried. "And here we are without an effective marshal. McAllister had no right to ride off into the blue like that. It's his job to be in town. Maybe if he'd been here, this would never have happened."

"You could be right, Homer," Drummond said. "How much faith do you have in the man?"

"Must say I took to him right off," the mayor replied. He cocked his head suspiciously. "You saying you don't trust him?"

"Wouldn't go as far as that," Drummond replied. "But I must admit he makes me a little uneasy. He has a violent reputation."

The mayor looked around him. "Maybe that's the kind of man this place needs after this mess."

A few minutes later, Drummond stepped out onto the street. Curiously, there had been no mention of the men who did this thing. Nobody had broached any suspicions. Maybe he should have mentioned the subject himself. He paused for a moment among the men outside the office, lost in thought, reaching a stogie from his pocket. There was a stir among the men surrounding him. He glanced up. They were staring down the street toward the creek.

"Who is it?" a man demanded.

"By God," said another, "it's McAllister."

Drummond started to push his way through the men.

"He's got a prisoner with him."

His heart started pounding. At last he had a clear view of the street. He stopped and stared, hands clenched.

A horseman rode slowly up the street on a tired horse. McAllister. Behind him came three led horses and on one of them rode a man with his hands tied behind his back. His hat was low over his face, but it looked very like Marve Little. It wasn't possible, Drummond thought. God-damn McAllister.

The two riders came closer. It was

Marve all right. Drummond shrank back in the crowd, not wanting Marve to see him.

McAllister rode up to the office, greeted the men there with a tired smile and stepped down from the saddle. Homer Touch rushed from the office and caught him by both arms.

"My God, McAllister, am I glad to see you," he cried.

"That's real nice, mayor."

The mayor blurted out all that had happened since McAllister had been out of town. McAllister didn't make any reply, but went and cut the bonds that held Marve's feet. He heaved the man out of the saddle and said: "We don't want anything to happen to you, do we, Marve? You heard what the mayor said? Frank's been shot. By your friends. The same thing could happen to you." He pushed Marve ahead of him and entered the office.

The first man he saw was Jim Carson lying, pale-faced, on the cot.

"Howdy, Jim."

"Howdy, Rem." Carson's eyes went past McAllister and rested on Marve. "So we still have one."

"We still have one." McAllister looked to the left and saw Pat O'Doran. He didn't miss the badge on his chest. "Nice to have you with us, Pat. Sorry you had such a warm reception."

Pat grinned a little.

"Sure, I'll live," he said.

"You get any of 'em?" McAllister demanded.

Carson said: "Must have hit at least one. Before Frank died he let go both barrels of a greener through the window in their faces."

McAllister looked at Marve. The man's face was grim and bitter.

McAllister walked to the cell and looked inside. On the cot in there lay the Texas cowhand. He didn't look too good.

"Hell," said McAllister, "can't we ever get rid of you, son."

The boy said: "I'm liable to sue you, Rem. I want compensation for this."

165

"You're gettin' free board an' lodgin's, ain't you? What more do you want."

"Just complainin' it gets awful noisy in the early hours," the boy said.

McAllister walked back into the office and said: "I'll ask all you good people to clear outa here now. This is a marshal's office not a hospital."

Emily Penshurst said: "That is the kind of thanks I'd expect to get from you, McAllister."

"Then I haven't disappointed you, ma'am."

He took hold of Marve and shoved him in the cell. The grill door clanged shut.

He told the man: "Set there an' think a mite. Think about how you can talk and save yourself from hangin'."

He turned and saw Will Drummond standing in the doorway. His face was pale and his eyes looked large and dark in his face. Drummond turned to Emily Penshurst and took her by the arm. "Come, my dear,' he said. "I'll take you home. My offer still stands, marshal."

As they walked out together, McAllister asked Carson: "What offer was that, Jim?"

"To take care of me at his house," Carson told him.

"Over my dead body," McAllister said. "You're a lawman an' you can still hold a gun, can't you? Pat, can you stand?"

"If I try real hard."

"Then try real hard an' get behind that desk and look official. You an' Jim're holdin' the fort while I'm out on the town."

The big Irishman set his teeth, sweated with the strain and the pain and got to his feet. Somebody came forward and offered to help him, but he shook off the helping hand with a curse. He reached the desk and fell into the chair behind it. McAllister picked up a greener from the rack and placed it on the desk. He took a bottle and glass from the cupboard and placed it at Pat's elbow. The Irishman looked appreciative and poured himself a drink. When he had done that, McAllister took a long pull from the bottle.

The young doctor came forward and

said: "These are two very sick men, Mr. McAllister."

McAllister said. "They're lawmen, doctor."

The young doctor picked up his bag and said: "I'll be around to see them this evening."

McAllister said: "Let me know if there're any gunshot wounds around town, doc."

The doctor nodded and left the office. Homer Touch said: "Are you going to find the men who perpetrated this terrible deed, McAllister."

"Reckon I am, mayor."

"Let it be soon," said the mayor. "Let it be very soon. None of us will feel safe in our beds before these murderers are brought to justice."

He departed.

McAllister checked his gun, took off his coat because the day was warm now and spoke to Marve.

"I hope you're thinkin', Marve. Thinkin' real hard. I'm right out of patience. They killed your brother. They gunned him down like he was no more'n an animal. Or is that what he was, an animal? Are you the same, without no feelin's? You got no feelin's? You don't feel a thing because Frank was murdered? You think about it. You just sit there and wonder whether you're a man or a yellow-livered coyote."

Marve said: "To hell with you."

McAllister went out onto the street. He gathered up the lines of his horses and walked up the street with them. He took them into the livery and gave precise instructions as to their care. To the livery owner he said: "I'll buy that dun from you. It'll do as crow bait when I get around to shootin' crows."

The man protested: "You won't see a horse as good as that for a long time."

"All right. Just remember, you sell him to anybody else an' I'll have your hide."

He walked off and angled across the street to the Golden Fleece. He might as well start here as anywhere. He had to throw a scare into the town and he would do it right off. He would have preferred a large steak and a long sleep, but there was a proper time for everything.

10

BEFORE he walked into the saloon, he braced himself. He couldn't remember when he had been so tired. He pushed open the door and saw that though it was mid-morning there was a goodly crowd there already. The herds were starting to come up from Texas and there were plenty of trail-drivers there drinking. Some just starting, some trying to get rid of hangovers from the night before. Everywhere he heard the Texas drawl. He felt at home.

He went up to the bar.

The fat barkeep said: "What's your pleasure, mister?"

"I don't have any this morning. Where's Fred an' Johnny?"

"Fred's in the office. I haven't seen Johnny."

McAllister walked the length of the bar, went through the doorway beyond and entered the long dark passage. He walked into the office and found Fred sitting at the table drinking. He looked three-parts drunk.

Fred said: "I didn't hear you knock."

McAllister ignored him and picked up the bottle.

"Got a glass?"

Fred jerked his head toward the sideboard. McAllister went over and picked up a glass. He poured himself some whiskey. He looked sideways at Darcy and thought he looked like a man who had been deeply shaken. There was something wrong here.

"You look like hell, Fred," he told the other.

Darcy didn't look at him.

"I feel like hell," he said. "Somethin' I ate."

"Where's Johnny?"

"What do you want to know where he's at for?"

"It's a simple question, it don't take much answering and I couldn't convict you on it."

Fred shot him a hard look from under his heavy brows.

"He ain't around."

"Where is he, Fred?"

"What makes you so interested in knowin' where Johnny's at all of a sudden?" Fred Darcy seemed to have come out of his daze. His dark eyes were alert, suspicious.

"I wasn't very interested, but I am now," McAllister told him.

"If you must know—he's gone home."

"To Texas?"

"That's where."

"Must of been somethin' pretty urgent to take Johnny back where there's a dozen lawmen waiting for him."

Fred stared at him hard for a moment, then said: "Ma sent for him. When Ma sends you go runnin'."

McAllister finished his whiskey and walked to the center of the room. He pushed back the couch with his foot.

"What's that on the floor there?" he asked abruptly, pointing down.

Fred looked.

"Where?"

"There."

"I don't see a thing."

McAllister looked at him hard.

"I see a spot of blood. Pretty fresh, too," he said. "You been hurt, Fred?"

"Me? No, I ain't been hurt. It can't be blood," Fred protested. "There ain't been nobody hurt around here."

"Johnny?"

"I told you. Didn't I tell you? He's on his way home to Texas."

McAllister turned and walked to the door. Once there he swung on Fred and said, pointing: "I'm goin' to nail you, Fred."

Darcy looked dangerous. It was an impressive sight and anybody is his senses took notice of it. His skill with a gun was known from one end of the frontier to the other. McAllister had confidence in his own ability to handle a gun, but he wouldn't have liked to bet on himself against the man.

"Don't push me too hard, son," Fred said. "I ain't the most peaceable man."

174

McAllister grinned suddenly.

"You'll be peaceable when I pin you, Fred." He opened the door, went out and shut it behind him. Fred found that he was sweating and shaking again. How much did that McAllister know?

McAllister walked into the bar and said to the barman: "You live on the premises?" The man said he did. "Where were you when the shooting started last night?"

"In my room above here."

"What did you do when the shooting woke you?"

"I got dressed and I went to see what was goin' on."

"Where was Fred Darcy at that time?"

"Mister, I work for Fred. He treats me right."

McAllister's smile was unpleasant. He said: "And I'm the law. If you don't answer my questions I'm goin' to lean on you—hard."

"You don't frighten me."

"I'll find a way. Now where was Fred when the shooting started?"

"In his room, I guess."

175

"And Johnny?"

The man looked scared now. The question had taken him off-balance.

"Johnny ain't in town."

"Where's he at?"

"He's gone to Texas."

"When did he go?"

"How should I know that. Mister, I only work here."

"That doesn't make you dumb and blind. So you can't say where Fred was at the time of the shooting?"

The man's face brightened. "I saw him down there in the crowd after. He must have run outa here about the same time I did."

"But you don't know for sure."

"I guess not."

McAllister nodded his thanks and walked out of the saloon. He was tireder than ever now, but he knew he wasn't finished yet. As he went through the door, he glanced back. Fred Darcy was at the corridor door and had seen him talking to the barkeep. Fred would be a

176

worried man now. The worrieder the better.

On the sidewalk, McAllister came face to face with Will Drummond.

"Howdy, Drummond."

The man stopped, smiling, pleasant, his hand outstretched.

"I must congratulate you, marshal," he said.

"What did I do?"

"You brought in Marve Little," Drummond said. "Everybody in town bet you wouldn't. That was a terrible thing that happened while you were out of town."

"What was that?"

Drummond looked surprised.

"Why the raid on the marshal's office, the killing of those two men," he said.

"Aw, that," said McAllister. "I ain't cryin'. Saved the hangman a chore, I reckon. Besides, it helped identify the men behind it and the men behind it were the same that raided the bank and killed Art Malloy."

Drummond's face was a picture. His jaw fell.

"You can't mean it, McAllister," he exclaimed.

"Sure, I mean it. Another twenty-four hours and I'll have the whole bunch of 'em nailed."

"Well . . . I know you're a confident man, but surely this is pushing confidence a little too far."

"You wanta bet?"

"I'm not a betting man."

McAllister laughed.

"Pity—a lawman's pay is pretty poor."

He lifted a hand and strolled on. Drummond stared after him. A sudden panic hit him. For a moment, he believed what the man told him. Then disbelief came. McAllister had to be bluffing. But what if it were true and McAllister did know the men who had killed Malloy, raided the bank and shot up the marshal's office? That didn't mean he knew that Drummond was in any way connected with the incidents. Drummond looked up and saw that he was outside the Golden Fleece. His mind froze . . . McAllister had just come from there. He had been talking to Fred Darcy. The dead Johnny . . .

Drummond looked around hastily. McAllister's back was squarely at him. Drummond quickly slipped into the alleyway and hurried along it. He let himself in the rear entrance of the saloon, went along the corridor and pushed into Darcy's office. It was empty. He cursed. He dare not go into the saloon for Darcy. He would have to wait.

He waited. It was almost thirty minutes before Darcy came in and his patience was stretched to the limit.

Darcy stared at him for a moment, then said: "Aw, it's you. What do you want?"

"I just talked to McAllister," Drummond said.

"So?"

"He was here questioning you."

"You couldn't hardly call it that."

"What would you call it?"

Darcy moved to the table and poured himself a drink. He was drinking more than was good for him, Drummond thought. He had never before seen such a sudden and terrible change in a man. Darcy was going to pieces. It was a terrible risk having him around. When he was himself, Drummond relied on him like he did no other man. He had nerves of steel, he could be ruthless. A first rate tool for Drummond to use. But now—the man had outlived his uses. He must leave town. But he would be hard to move out. He had too much at stake, too much to lose. Everything he had in the world was here in town, in this saloon. But Drummond would find a way to move him and he would find a way to profit from it as well. With all the witnesses against him out of the way, he could start again in a stronger positon than ever. This storm of violence would pay off better than he had ever dreamed.

Darcy was saying: "He's marshal. It's his job to nose around. It don't mean nothin'."

"Did he ask about Johnny?"

Darcy's painfilled eyes met Drummond's. He was reluctant to answer, but he did. Drummond still had some mysterious power over him.

"Yeah, he did. I told him the kid's gone home to Texas."

"And did he swallow that?"

"I reckon."

Drummond rested back on the couch, the couch on which the dead Johnny had lain so short a time before. He put his fingertips together. His hands were very white and soft.

"As I told you," he said, "I just talked with McAllister. He suspects you, Fred. I've come to you as a friend with your interest at heart. I owe you more than I could owe any man. I don't want to see you pay for everything we have all done."

Darcy scowled.

"What the hell's that supposed to mean? Why should McAllister suspect me?" he demanded fiercely.

"I don't know precisely," Drummond said thoughtfully. "It must have been something that happened here? What exactly did happen?"

181

"Nothin' . . . Christ! *It was the blood!*"

Drummond sat bolt upright.

"Blood?"

Darcy pointed.

"There was a spot on the floor there. Johnny's."

"My God," said Drummond, springing to his feet, "I knew it was bad, but I didn't know it was that bad."

"He can't prove a thing."

"Fred—he told me he was going to arrest you within twenty-four hours."

Darcy had not been frightened many times in his life, but he was as close as he had ever been now. Johnny getting killed, the drink . . . McAllister coming here; now Drummond . . . He was confused.

"I ain't scared of McAllister," he said.

Drummond said: "It isn't a matter of being scared. It's a matter of using your head. You've got a lot to lose, Fred. You've built this place up and it's made you a lot of money."

"I don't aim to lose this. I'll kill McAllister first," Fred declared.

"There's a lot of risk involved. As I said, you have a lot to lose now. I know what I'd do if I were in your boots."

"What?"

"Cut my losses. You must have a good pile in the bank now. I'd sell and light out for Montana, California, anywhere where I'm not known."

Darcy eyed him. He looked wary, as well he might.

"You sayin' I should sell out?" he demanded.

"Fred, listen to me . . . you've got to run. McAllister is coming for you as sure as God made little apples. You want to run and lose the value of this place?"

Darcy put his head down in his hands, fingers working in his hair. When he looked up his eyes were wild.

"You've got me over a barrel, Drummond, an' you know it, God damn you."

"Don't put it that way, Fred. We're friends. I want to help. You need me. How else're you going to get your money from the bank. You'll want a fast horse. You'll want to sell this place. I'll give you a fair price for it."

Darcy looked like a lost and wounded bear, not knowing which way to turn.

"I know what the place is worth," he almost shouted. "You ain't gettin' nothin' cheap from me, Drummond."

Drummond allowed the tone of his voice to alter slightly. Enough to put a little coldness into it.

"You're a good business man, Fred. You have been till now. Let's be practical. You can't get this place bought by anybody but me and you know it. You sell to anybody else and McAllister will hear it."

Darcy's anger started to show plainly.

"So this is the barrel you got me over."

"This is business. I'm not a sentimentalist."

"This place is worth every cent of ten thousand."

Drummond looked aghast.

"Ten thousand? You must be out of your mind. I'll be frank, under these circumstances I wouldn't give you more than three for it."

Darcy looked so savage that, for a moment, Drummond thought the man was going to hurl himself at him. His hand flicked inside his coat and gripped the butt of the pocket gun.

"You tryin' to steal me blind," Darcy shouted. "You know what? I'd druther burn the place down than give it you at that price."

Drummond knew the man meant it. It was just the kind of highly emotional thing he would do.

Drummond allowed himself a smile. He wanted Darcy cooled off.

"All right," he said. "For a friend, I'll add a thousand. I'm being generous. I'll make it up to four thousand for old time's sake. I wouldn't do it for any other man."

"You'd rob your grandmother and raise your hat while you did it," Darcy growled. "Four thousand's a joke and you know it. You're wastin' your breath. I'll not come below seven thousand. I'm givin' it away at that price."

185

Drummond shook his head regretfully.

"Sorry, Fred, it's no deal. We'd best leave it. Forget it." He turned to the door. "I'll see you get your money from the bank. I'll arrange for a good horse to be delivered to the rear door. When are you going?"

"I ain't said I'm goin' yet."

"All right, please yourself. Forget the whole thing." He opened the door.

"Hold up," Darcy said.

Drummond turned back.

"Make it six and you have a deal."

Drummond shook his head again. "There's only another season to go in this town. I'd never get the money back. I'll meet you at five."

"Christ!" Fred breathed through his teeth. "You're a hard bastard, Drummond." The man in the doorway waited patiently. He would pay the price he had reckoned on. "All right, it's a deal."

"I'm glad you saw sense. I'll go straight to the bank and make arrangements. When do you want the horse?"

186

Darcy thought. Finally, he said:
"Midnight tonight."

"Right."

Drummond left.

Fred Darcy stood thinking how he would like to kill him. One day . . .

11

McALLISTER sloped into a restaurant. It was almost empty. A little Mexican girl waited on him. He demanded a large steak, eggs, fried potatoes, coffee. Make it enough for two. The girl flounced her hips at him and later brought him what he wanted. He ate his way steadily through the feast and when it was under his belt he felt considerably better. He paid, slapped the waitress on the behind and tramped back to the office. Pat O'Doran sat behind the desk still with the shotgun in front of him. McAllister told him that he was going to get some sleep.

Jim Carson asked: "How's it goin'?"

"So-so."

McAllister made his bed up on the floor and was asleep in seconds.

Drummond arranged Darcy's affairs at

the bank. Penshurst didn't like it, but what he liked didn't matter any more. The banker asked questions, but Drummond evaded him. He walked back to the saloon, entered by the rear door and found Darcy again. The Texan was subdued now, surly, still drinking. Drummond didn't like the look of him and wondered if he would cut up rough. He was rather surprised to find some of the fight gone out of Darcy.

"What's the talk in the town?" he asked.

"That McAllister's going to make an arrest."

Darcy seemed to search the room for an answer to that. He didn't find it. His eyes came back to Drummond.

"I can't get outa here till dark."

Drummond said confidently: "You'll be all right if you go tonight. I've arranged everything at the bank."

"Did Penshurst ask questions?"

"Yes, but I didn't answer them. Don't worry about him. He'll keep his mouth shut." He had a bulging envelope on the table. Darcy opened it and glanced through the contents, grunting as he did so. When he finished, he said: "That looks all right."

"The papers for this place," Drummond said.

"They're here." They spent the next ten minutes going over them. They signed. Drummond handed over the money. Only then did Darcy cheer up. The sight of it seemed like magic.

"You'll find me in San Francisco if you want me," he said. "The best of everythin' for a while."

Drummond put the papers in his pocket. He felt good.

"I'll bring the horse personally at midnight," he said. "I'll tie in the shadow of that tree behind your loading platform."

"Is it good?"

"The best."

Drummond held out his hand. Darcy hesitated for a moment, then gripped the other's hand hard.

"We had a good run for our money," he said.

"Goodbye, Fred, and the best of luck."

Drummond turned and went from the room. In the alleyway, he paused. Now there was only Marve to worry about and he wasn't a man who talked easily. But McAllister might be a man who made it hard for a man not to talk. McAllister was an Indian through and through. Drummond estimated the man as being able to make stone talk.

He didn't know what he was going to do about Marve. But he knew what he was going to do about Darcy. It was risky, but there had been risk in all the profit he had made in the past and he had won through.

That evening he dined with Emily Penshurst and her father, with Clarissa waiting at table. She put on a very fine dinner with wine at a perfect temperature. During the dinner, Drummond was gay, suave and entertaining. Emily Penshurst didn't know when she had spent a happier or more stimulating evening. She was almost reconciled to the fact of marrying a man she wasn't in love with. She could do a lot worse than Will Drummond. Certainly other women would envy her. She would have everything any woman could want. Drummond was a good-looking man with an easy manner and a great kindliness. He was attentive and gave as much consideration to her opinions as he would if she had been a man. Her father too seemed to have softened toward Will. The men chatted amiably. Drummond may have taken over the bank, but he seemed to treat the older man with every consideration. At one point he even went so far as to say "we" when he referred to his future operations. Laughingly, he said: "Mr. Penshurst, with your experience and my nerve, there's nothing we couldn't accomplish. But we must look forward. This town can't last forever. There's a fortune to be made by the men ready to change their locations quick enough and at the right time. Buying and selling in towns is like handling shares. You won't make a cent if you don't buy and sell at the right moment."

"I couldn't agree with you more," Penshurst said.

They smoked cigars together. Penshurst told them tales from his early years. Drummond seemed to find them interesting and highly entertaining. Penshurst seemed to blossom. They stayed late and left with regret. When he closed the door behind them, Drummond went into the kitchen where the woman was sewing at the table.

"We own the Golden Fleece" he said.

"How much did it cost?"

"I'll tell you that when I know for sure," he told her.

McAllister awoke. Pat had lit the lamps in the office. There was a pump at the rear of the building and McAllister put his head under that for a few minutes. He felt a little better then. He fetched food from the restaurant for the prisoners and the law. He ate in the office himself. The Texas cowhand objected to being in the same cell as Marve Little. McAllister told him there was no other in town and if he was fussy about his cell-mates he shouldn't wear a gun in a town with only one cell. Marve was quiet.

"Tomorrow," McAllister said. "We'll talk, Marve. Or you'll talk."

"We don't have nothin' to talk about," Marve growled. "Me an' Frank . . . you reckon we gunned down Malloy because he killed our brother. You prove it."

"I ain't interested. I can't prove that without much trouble. I want you for the bank robbery."

Marve looked a little surprised.

"You can't tie me in with that."

"I don't have to tie you in with anythin', if you talk. I want the man behind the bank raid. Give me that an' I could forget an awful lot. Frank's dead. I reckon that could make the Malloy balance right."

Carson objected explosively—

"I'll have something to say about that."

McAllister told him: "You keep outa this. You're sick. I'm actin' marshal."

"Then what the hell am I doin' here?"

"Restin'."

Marve said: "If I had somethin' to tell you, I'd talk. But I don't have. You can use the boot on me an' it wouldn't make no difference."

"We'll come to that tomorrow," McAllister said. He turned back into the office. "Pat, if you can crawl to the door, drop the bar behind me. I'm goin' out. Maybe I'll be out all night."

"Where you goin'?" Carson wanted to know.

"I'm goin' to catch a rat," McAllister told him and walked out of the office.

It was dark on the street; a few lamps burned here and there; the saloons were going full swing. There was a lot of noise, shouting and music. There was little wheeled traffic, but there were plenty of people on foot. McAllister walked down Main and reached the creek. Here he turned along the footpath, threaded his way through the thick brush and came up eventually south of town. Working his way through the brush, he came to the

195

rear of the Golden Fleece. There was no mistaking the place: lights were on and there was plenty of noise. Somebody was punishing an out-of-tune piano and several men were singing discordantly. McAllister stayed in the cover of the brush for a short while. A man came out of the rear door of the saloon and threw something made of glass amongst the trash in the empty ground. He hawked and spat, silhouetted starkly against the light from the door, stretched, yawned and walked back in, slamming the door behind him. McAllister broke cover, drifted through the darkness and trash, ducked down and slid himself under the loading platform. He took some tobacco from his pocket and stuffed it in his cheek. There was a long wait ahead of him, maybe.

He was there a couple of hours before he heard anything. During that time, a cat came and rubbed itself against him and a dog sniffed him out. The cat fled from the dog, the dog fled from McAllister when the man showed hostility.

The sound that aroused him was a horse walking roughly from the direction from which he had come himself. Some twenty yards in front of him was the tall and spreading form of a tree. The sound of the horse seemed to stop at the foot of this. McAllister strained his eyes, but he could only dimly make out the form of the man. There was a pause of a few moments, during which McAllister guessed the man was tying the horse. Then the man moved away, going west. Quickly, he was lost in the darkness. Once he walked into a shaft of light from a window, but the moment of revelation was too brief for McAllister to recognise the man.

All was quiet, except for the row in the saloon. Nothing stirred in the backlots. Thirty minutes passed. A door opened above McAllister. It closed. Silence. Then bootheels sounded on the planks above him. The man walked to the edge of the platform right above McAllister, jumped to the ground and walked toward the horse. He walked like a man laden, kicking his way through the trash. He reached the horse and McAllister interpreted the sounds of that of a man loading a horse. This was followed by the creak of leather as the man mounted.

McAllister heaved himself from under the loading platform and drew the Remington. The rider and horse moved away from the tree. Lamplight from the buildings touched them faintly.

McAllister called out: "Hold it right there, Fred, or I'll blast you."

The horse came to a standstill. The saddle creaked as the man turned.

Fred Darcy said calmly: "Damn you, McAllister—I thought I was in the clear."

McAllister's mind told him: *He's too calm. He's going to try something.* His muscles and nerves tautened for a quick shot.

A faint sound came from behind him. He started to turn. Something hit him hard on the base of the skull. The ground leaped up violently and struck him in the face. He fought to rise, to roll, but another blow came and pitched him onto his face.

Will Drummond walked toward Fred Darcy.

"It's all right, Fred," he said quietly. "I've settled McAllister."

Darcy said: "Thanks, Drummond. That's real neighbourly of you."

Drummond came up and kept the nervous horse still by holding onto the bridle.

"I'll say goodbye again," he said. "The road's clear all the way to California now. I'd best move on before the law awakes." He laughed.

"Luck to you," Darcy said.

"There's just one other thing, Fred, before you go," Drummond said.

"What's that?"

"This."

Drummond shot the pocket revolver out at armslength, cocked and fired.

Darcy fell back over the cantle, seemed to stay for a moment on the rump of the horse and fell to the ground almost at

Drummond's feet. Drummond released the suddenly panic-stricken horse now and it jumped forward into the brush. Drummond thrust the gun away and hastily went through the pockets of the dead man, finding what he wanted in the inside pocket of the jacket. He put these in his own pocket and got to his feet, turning and running as fast as he could go into the brush. He ran west, the brush tearing at his clothes until he reckoned that he was opposite his own street. Then he turned down an alleyway, reached the street and walked along it, hoping that his disheveled appearance would pass muster in the poor light. He let himself into his kitchen. The woman was still there, sewing. She looked up and her expression didn't change. Did she ever show an emotion? he asked himself.

"You look like you had yourself quite a time," she said.

"You asked me how much the Golden Fleece cost," he said, a twisted smile marking his unnaturally pale face. "Nothing. It didn't cost us a cent."

"Good," she said. "I hope you don't have to pay for it later."

"What's that supposed to mean?" he demanded, nettled.

"There's been violence." He nodded. "There's been a deal too much lately. You could pay for it with your life."

"And you wouldn't weep a single tear."

"Not a single tear."

He walked out of the room and went up to his own. He found a bottle of whiskey there and drank deeply. Killing a man always made him a little sick in the stomach. He washed carefully, got into his night clothes and got into bed. He thought that he would not be able to find sleep for hours, but he was asleep in minutes.

His last thought was that he was a pretty smart man. He hadn't been able to risk a shot on McAllister because there wouldn't have been time to kill Darcy and get away. Maybe he should have taken the extra risk and gone back and killed McAllister after. But he thought not. He had showed a good profit as it was.

12

McALLISTER was dimly aware that there were men all around him. When he opened his eyes, the light of a lamp bit into them. He could see men's boots, above them faces; he heard his name. The world was composed of a head-splitting pain. He wanted to retch, but was ashamed to do so in front of so many men.

"Wa-al," said one man, "he's alive for sure."

"This one's dead," a more distant voice shouted. "Shot plumb through the heart."

McAllister tried to sit up. Somebody must have carved his skull with an axe.

"Who's dead?" he demanded and his voice was no more than a croak.

One of the men near him shouted: "Who is it, Jake?"

The answering shout came back: "Fred Darcy."

The men said the name, savoring it, realising that the famous Texan gunfighter had at last met his comeuppence. They were astonished and grave.

Hands helped McAllister to his feet. He thought: *Darcy dead. Me with a split head. Some bastard's goin' to pin this on me.*

"Find my gun," he said.

The man with the lamp started to search around.

"Here it is," said a man.

McAllister didn't put a hand for it.

"Look at it," he said. "Smell it." The man obeyed. "Have him check you." Another man took the gun, smelled the muzzle, checked the loads. "Has it been fired?"

"No, sir. This gun ain't bin fired."

"You agree with that."

"Sure do, marshal."

"Right, thanks." He took the gun from them and thrust it away into the holster. He staggered a little as he walked and his head throbbed almost unbearably. He felt like he was going to fall on his face at any moment.

Another lamp burned under the tree. The young doctor was down on one knee beside the dead body of Fred Darcy. He looked up as McAllister came up.

"How do you feel?" he asked.

"Like hell," McAllister told him.

"Well, Darcy's dead all right. Did you shoot him?"

"No," said McAllister, "but I'd like to know the man who did. Doc, do you think you could dig the bullet out that killed him?"

The doctor cocked his head. "It's in pretty deep, but I'll get it out if it helps you at all."

"I'm grateful."

"You go and get some rest."

"Marshal and deputy wounded, a murderer skulking around town and you tell me to get some rest."

"It's what you need."

McAllister patted the young man on the shoulder and said: "Thanks anyway." He walked back through the men gathered at the rear of the saloon and wondered about Fred Darcy. He was lighting out all right, but he wouldn't have done that without selling the saloon. McAllister would like to know who he sold it to. Abruptly, he turned around and walked back to the dead man. The others watched him as he dropped on one knee and went through the man's pockets. Nothing.

"Did anybody ketch his horse?"

"Sure, it's over yonder."

McAllister walked over to the horse and searched in the saddlepockets. There were some changes of clothing and some supplies. Nothing else. He untied the bedroll and opened it. Nothing there. Fred Darcy had been a comparatively wealthy man and here he was leaving town without a cent on him, bar the loose change in his pockets. The whole thing smelled.

Slowly, he walked back to the office, knocked and called and after a fairly long delay the door was opened. Pat O'Doran said: "The wanderer returns." McAllister stepped into the lamplight and the Irishman said: "Jesus! What in the holy name happened to youse?"

"I was clobbered. But good."

Pat said: "I have the very cure for that right here."

He found the whiskey bottle and handed it to McAllister, who took a good pull and felt a bit better. He took another pull and felt better still.

Five minutes later the mayor appeared fluffing and huffing, telling McAllister that things looked bad for him and he didn't know what view the judge was going to take of the affair. Things seemed to have gone from bad to worse since Malloy had been killed. McAllister told him that if he wasn't satisfied with what he was doing, he had better get himself another marshal. The mayor took a drink and changed his tone a little. He was a very worried man. He didn't want any more killings in his town. Already the eastern newspapers were saying bad things about his town.

The mayor departed and the young

doctor arrived. He had dug the bullet out of Darcy. He handed it to McAllister who inspected it and passed it on to Carson. The marshal pursed his lips and said: "Thirty-eight."

"That let's me out," McAllister said. The doctor picked up his case and went. His head aching like hell, his temper short, McAllister spent an hour with Marve trying to make him talk, trying every angle he knew, but he didn't get anywhere. He decided to sleep and did so.

He awoke at dawn, took a wash, shaved and felt a little more human, but his head still ached like a fury. He inspected his wounded—Pat said he felt fine, just fine and he'd be skipping in a couple of days. McAllister walked over to the restaurant and fetched breakfast from the little Mexican girl for his wounded and the prisoners. After he had eaten well himself —a plate of ham and three eggs washed down with a pot of coffee. He felt even better then. He carried the tray back to the office and watched the others eat. The

Texas cowhand was looking chastened and Marve was sullen.

"Feel like talkin', Marve?" McAllister asked.

"Go to hell."

"Watch out somebody don't come through the door and gun you down like they did Frank."

Marve gave him a deadly look and turned away.

McAllister left Pat in charge, shotgun on desk and walked over to the Golden Fleece. There was a swamper at work and the barkeep McAllister had spoken to before was smoking a cigar and watching the swamper lugubriously. There was one or two drinks left over from the night before, but otherwise the place was empty.

"Mornin'," said McAllister.

"Mornin'."

"What happens now?"

"What's that supposed to mean?"

"Your boss is dead. Who owns this place now?"

"How should I know? I only work here."

McAllister said: "I'll take a look around the office."

"I wouldn't do that if I was you."

"You aim to stop me?"

"Don't get me wrong, marshal. Hell, all I meant was . . . well, the owner . . . There must be an owner."

McAllister smiled.

"He'll turn up. You'll see."

McAllister walked through the bar into the office.

He spent the next thirty minutes going through Fred Darcy's desk. Darcy had not been the tidiest of men, nor had he been methodical in any way. The place was a mess, but McAllister learned few things about Darcy he hadn't known before. He had been mixed up in cattle deals, which may or may not have been straight; he had run some women down on the line, west of town; he had lent money at exorbitant rates. McAllister decided the only nice thing about the man was his whiskey. He sat down on the couch, put his feet on the table and sipped from the bottle. This wasn't the rubbish sold to the customers out front. This was the real McCoy. McAllister was fully appreciative of the fact.

He dozed a little, drank a little and started to forget his headache.

The door opened and a man entered.

McAllister looked at him through lowered lashes. It was Will Drummond.

Drummond said in a cool gentle voice: "May I ask what the meaning of this is?"

McAllister hadn't seen this side of the man before and it interested him. He drank deeply from the bottle, belched and said: "Mornin'."

"I asked you a question, marshal."

McAllister drank again and put the bottle down on the table. He placed his feet on the floor and stood up.

"An' I'll ask you a question. What the hell's it got to do with you?"

"I happen to own this place."

McAllister grinned broadly.

"I've been waitin' here forcin' your whiskey down me to find that out."

Drummond pursed his lips.

"It's no secret. It was a piece of legitimate trading. Darcy wanted to leave town and he came to me with an offer."

"I'll bet it was to your advantage with him on the run an' all," McAllister offered.

"I'm a business man."

"It must have given you quite a turn seein' me waitin' here."

"Not at all. It annoyed me a little to see you making yourself at home with your feet on my table."

McAllister walked past him to the door and turned. He had a feeling about this man. There was something here he didn't like. He hadn't liked it the first time he had seen Drummond.

"You'll find I'm goin' to annoy you a whole lot before I'm done, Drummond," he said.

"I'm not at all sure I like your tone, marshal," Drummond said. "There's an implied threat in it."

"You're not goin' to like anythin' about me before long," McAllister told him.

"You're goin' to hate my guts. You're the smooth smilin' boy in this town, Drummond. You're the nice-mannered eligible bachelor all the girls hanker after and the mothers swoon over. But I think that underneath that nice outside there's a rotten inside."

"Good God, man," Drummond said, "what kind of a marshal are you, talking this way? This could be the finish of you. This is libel of the worst order."

"There ain't nobody here but us two, an' you wouldn't spread it around the nasty marshal called you a nasty man," McAllister said.

Drummond changed his tack.

"Look, Mr. McAllister," he said, "I don't know what started this, but we seem to have gotten off on the wrong foot together. Let's start afresh."

"Let's not," said McAllister. "Let's stay nice and unfriendly. Then when I hang you I shan't feel so bad about it."

"Hang me?" Drummond cried, looking as though he were astonished out of his wits. "What in heaven's name are you saying?"

"I'm sayin' I'll hang you before I'm through, Drummond," McAllister informed him coolly. "I have a nose for skunks like you an' I ain't never wrong."

"What am I supposed to have done? What led up to this crazy talk? I don't know what notion you have in your head about me, but I swear I have no idea what you're talking about."

McAllister leaned in the doorway, filling it.

"I ain't tellin' you a thing, Drummond," he said. "You sweat awhile. You or one of your boys'll have to get me from a dark alley if'n you want to stop me. So just sweat and think up all the ways you can of killin' me without leaving a trace. You'll need to be good. You won't get me like Malloy or Frank Little was got."

"You mean you think I'm connected with those foul murders? You must be out of your mind."

"'Sright. I'm real crazy. Just watch the crazy things I do. You'll die laughin'."

McAllister turned away.

Drummond listened to the sound of his bootfalls dying away through the saloon. He found that he was shaking. McAllister had said he would let him sweat. To his disgust he found that he *was* sweating. *Damn the man*. He had challenged him. He had dared him to try and kill him. He'd kill him all right. He shoot him in the guts and watch him die, he'd laugh in his face as he writhed in agony for the last time. God damn him to hell.

He reached out for the whiskey bottle on the table and found to his disgust that McAllister had finished it. He cursed insanely and flung the bottle across the room. Searching in the cupboard on the far side of the room, he found another, removed the cork and drank deeply.

He sat down and tried to think. Slowly, he regained command of himself. The situation looked dangerous. McAllister couldn't have anything to go on, but he was a reckless man and therefore dangerous. Instinctively, Drummond knew that here was a man who didn't work by the book. McAllister wasn't orthodox and he didn't care.

So, what had to be done?

There must be more killings. First, though he was tempted to kill McAllister, he knew he must kill Marve Little. If Marve talked, he could kill McAllister ten times over and it wouldn't prevent a rope from going around his neck.

How to kill Marve?

Try the simple way first.

He drank again and smiled to himself. It was going to take a smarter man than McAllister to stop William Drummond.

13

THEY sat or lay around in the office, smoking, drinking coffee, occasionally talking. The judge had come and gone. A peppery old number with years of administering some kind of law on a rough frontier. He hadn't been very clean, nor very coherent, nor very sober for that matter, but his judgment had been sound enough. It was he who had insisted in holding court in the office. He didn't want any more shooting. The Texas cowhand he had set free with a ten dollar fine for carrying a gun within the town limits. He had done no more than question McAllister about Marve Little and told the defending attorney that Marve was a villain and he had better have a good case or else. Such behavior may not have been ethical, but it was to the point and Marve was sitting in the single cell looking pretty disheartened right now. McAllister had said that he would have his case against Marve complete in the next few days. The judge declared that the prisoner should be kept on ice for that period, the attorney objected, the judge told him to mind his own Goddamn business. When judge and defense retired, the prosecuting attorney, a middle-aged man about as sober as the judge, stayed behind to discuss Marve's case with McAllister, but they didn't get very far because McAllister didn't feel like discussing it. So the lawyer hurried off to the Golden Fleece for his mid-morning pickmeup.

Carson said: "You don't expect to pin this bastard, do you, Rem?"

McAllister said: "I'll pin the one who killed Malloy and Frank."

"How?"

"I ain't too sure of that. All I know is I'll do it. I feel it in my water."

Pat roared: "A premonition, by God. Nothin' likelier, me laddo."

They tossed the subject this way and that, but it didn't get them anywhere. Pat suggested McAllister bought them a bottle to while away the time. McAllister drifted down Main and came back with a bottle. But he didn't drink. He was too depressed. He liked to drink seriously when he felt good. If he drank when he felt bad it made him feel like hell. He lay on the floor dozing and thinking. He made his rounds in the evening. The town was pretty full of trail riders among whom he knew more than a few. He took a couple of drinks in two different saloons, received news of Texas and wandered back to the office. Come supper time, he went down the street and fetched a tray of food from the restaurant and fed marshals and prisoner. He didn't feel like eating himself, Pat ate as if he hadn't had a meal in weeks. McAllister and Carson twigged him idly about it. After the meal, Pat took some exercise up and down the office and swore that he'd be running in a couple of days. McAllister collected the dishes in the office, put them on the tray and went over to the cell.

"Push 'em out under the door, Marve," he told the prisoner.

Marve looked up from where he was sitting on the cot. He put the mug from which he had been drinking onto the clean plate and pushed them with his foot under the cell door. McAllister bent down. As his hand touched the plate he heard the gun come to full cock. Looking up, he saw the gun in Marve's hand.

"Take it easy, Mack," Marve said.

"Don't call me Mack," McAllister told him.

He straightened up and knew he was as near death as he could ever get. It wasn't a nice feeling. Carson screwed himself around on the bed so he could see better.

"Holy Mother," Pat said.

"Anybody looks at me wrong an' McAllister gets it," Marve told them. "Unbuckle your gunbelt and be awfully careful how you do it, McAllister."

McAllister unbuckled his belt. Holster, gun and belt thudded on the floor.

"Kick 'em this way," Marve said. McAllister obeyed. Not taking his eyes from the man in front of him, Marve bent down and pulled the Remington from leather with his left hand. "Now, let me outa here."

McAllister said: "I don't have the key."

"Where's it at?"

"On the hook yonder."

Marve said: "Fetch it, Pat. Take it real easy now or McAllister's dead."

The big Irishman stepped across the room and lifted the large keyring down from the hook.

Marve said: "Take one step to your right, McAllister," and was obeyed. Pat approached the cell and placed the key in the lock. In a moment, Marve stepped out into the office. He was in a highly nervous state and he showed it. He was sweating and his eyes were wild. McAllister knew that he would shoot if he were looked at wrong. He prayed that Carson and Pat would behave themselves. He hadn't planned to die just yet.

"You're bein' a damn fool, Marve," he said. "You know you can't get far."

"You'll never put a rope around my neck," Marve said.

"I know that. You'll be dead before you can get out of town. Whoever passed you that gun wants you dead like he wanted Frank dead."

Marve wavered for a moment.

"Save your breath," he said, "you ain't talkin' me back into that cell. Now, don't nobody come after me or they're mutton. Hear?"

He circled around them, facing them all the time and backed toward the door. Thrusting McAllister's gun under his belt, he felt back for the bar of the door with his left hand, lifted it and opened the door. He seemed to hesitate then, his gun still pointed at McAllister, till, taking a deep breath, he tore the door wide, turned and ran out onto the street.

For a moment, the fleeing prisoner found himself in the circle of light that came from the lamp hanging above the office door. Again, he hesitated, not knowing whether to go right or left. He wanted a

222

horse . . . more than anything he wanted a horse. The saloon would have horses hitched in front of it. He started right.

He heard the rush of movement behind him in the office and turning, he threw a shot through the open door.

A voice from across the street, startled him into motionlessness.

"Halt or I fire."

He crouched, strained his eyes and could see nothing but the dark bulk of the lightless buildings across the way. He triggered a shot off in the general direction of the sound of the voice. A window collapsed with a crash of glass.

A rifle slammed flatly.

The bullet thudded into the wall of the office and Marve ran.

The rifle was fired again.

Something knocked Marve sideways and he tripped on his own feet. He went down hard, but the fight hadn't gone out of him. Marve would die fighting. The will to survive was strong in him. He cocked and fired at a moving shadow.

Somebody thundered out of the

marshal's office and roared: "Hold your fire."

The rifle slammed again.

Marve in the act of driving himself to his feet, was hit in the heart. He went down without a sound, kicked twice and lay still.

McAllister stayed still for a moment, his eyes unaccustomed to the dim light of the street. He could see the dim form of Marve Little giving its tiny death kick. A man walked across from the other side of the street. He carried a rifle in his hands. McAllister waited until the light of the lamp fell on his face. It was Will Drummond.

Drummond halted in the middle of the road.

McAllister walked to the dead man, rolled him over and took his own gun from his belt. When he straightened up, he turned to gaze for a moment at Drummond before he pushed the gun away into its holster.

He strolled past Drummond and said: "Come into the office."

As McAllister entered the office, Carson and Pat watched him bug-eyed.

"What happened?" Carson asked. He was sitting up on the bed with his gun in his hand.

"Marve got himself shot," McAllister told him.

"You didn't shoot him."

"No, I didn't shoot him."

Drummond walked in.

"It was lucky I was there," he said. "Or he'd have got away."

"Real lucky," McAllister said coldly. "How did you just happen to be there?"

"Why, I was in the bank opposite."

"Kind of late to be callin' in at the bank, isn't it? Penshurst would have gone home long gone."

"I have an interest in the bank myself. I have a right to be there."

That interested McAllister. He thought about it while he listened to the sounds of the street. Folks were running along the street. Voices were raised. They had reached the body and were no doubt now staring at it with curiosity.

"With a rifle," McAllister said.

Drummond started.

"We keep the weapon at the bank for protection," he said. "After the raid, we thought it best."

"You go home, Mr. Drumond," McAllister told him. "I'll write a report on the affair and get you to sign it in the mornin'. I reckon the judge'll want a word with you too."

"I'll come down first thing in the morning. Anything to oblige."

He told them good evening and went out. McAllister followed him onto the sidewalk.

"I give you credit, Drummond," he said. "That was real neat. It's fooled everybody. Everybody that is except me."

Drummond said: "I don't know what you mean."

"Marve's dead. There isn't a chance he'll talk now."

"I would have thought you'd be

226

grateful, McAllister," Drummond said. "I stoped a man escaping."

"You stopped a man livin'."

"The town will be grateful if you're not. In fact, you'll look a bit of a fool. Little managing to get away like that."

McAllister said: "He had a gun. I'll find out how he got it."

Drummond smiled.

"You haven't done very well since you put on the badge, have you, McAllister? A bank raid and a prisoner escaped. I think the town could do without you."

McAllister watched the people gathered around the dead body. Carrion around dead game.

"I told you this morning," he said softly, "I'll hang you, Drummond. That still stands."

"You'd better be careful how you step," Drummond said. "I could get you run out of town."

McAllister said: "You can run me to California. I'd come back and get you."

Drummond walked off down the street, skirting the men around Marve's body.

McAllister walked that way, too, shouldered his way through the men and searched around for the gun Marve had had. He found it. It was a Colt pocket model, caliber .38. The same size that had killed Fred Darcy. Which didn't really prove a thing. He dropped it into his pocket and asked a man to fetch the undertaker.

Emily Penshurst was still up when Drummond reached the Penshurst place. She told him that her father had just gone up to bed. She would fetch him.

"No," Drummond told her, "it's you I want to see."

They went into the parlor where a lamp burned. He noted that the curtains were drawn. He turned to her and said: "I know I shouldn't be here this time of night, but I had to see you."

She saw that his face was drawn and pale.

"Your face," she said. "Has something happened?"

He sat down, genuinely tired. It was as if the whole of his strength had left him.

"Something terrible," he said.

She came and sat beside him, put her hands on his arm. Suddenly, she was frightened. So much had happened lately; she felt insecure. Her future had seemed assured, now she was scared that something would happen that would wreck it.

"Tell me," she said.

He hesitated for a moment, wondering how best to play his hand. Her touch stirred him; he could feel the warmth of her body beside him. Suddenly, he wanted her, wanted for a moment to forget the tension and the fear that were growing in him.

"I killed a man."

She started back from him, her eyes wide.

"My God . . . Do you mean you'll be arrested?" So it had come. The end of all her plans and hopes. She had picked the best man in town, the man with the brightest future and now this.

He smiled wanly.

"Oh, no," he said. "I shan't be arrested. It was all legal and above board."

"What happened?"

"I was at the bank. I heard a commotion from the marshal's office. It was Marve Little escaping. I challenged him and he fired at me. I had no alternative but to shoot. It was him or me."

She laughed shakily.

"I thought you meant you had committed murder," she said. "You have done your duty, that is all."

"Just the same . . . I've killed a man."

Her hands were on his arm again, her breasts were pressed against him.

"Don't let it be on your conscience," she told him. "The man was a criminal. He would have died anyway. There wasn't anything else you could have done. You mustn't blame yourself."

"I'm not a violent man," he said. "I hate violence."

"I know," she said. "You're the gentlest and kindest man I've ever known."

230

He gave her a grateful look, she smiled and kissed him on the cheek. He turned and put his arms around her; her arms went around his neck.

"We shouldn't," she said.

He kissed her on the mouth and her arms tightened. She fell back onto the couch with him almost on top of her. For a moment, she struggled against him, but the protest was no more than a gesture. Her mouth opened and his tongue slipped through her parted lips. She clung to him now, aroused.

When he took his mouth from hers, she panted: "No, no." He renewed his attack and her fervor matched his. His right hand fumbled at the neck of her dress and met the warm softness of her breast.

"I love you," he told her.

McAllister was tired, but he sat at the desk with his pipe going like a small furnace and carefully penned his report of what had happened. He was no great shakes with a pen, but he found that committing the incident to paper helped clear his mind. As he went on he warmed to the task and found by the time he finished that he had not done badly. Anybody reading it would suspect how he felt about Drummond. He knew that it would help to slowly swing the responsible opinion in town against the man. Every little helped. He was getting Drummond rattled and pretty soon the man would make a mistake. Then he would nail him.

He went to sleep with a feeling of satisfaction. He was not a man to dwell on his failures. Marve Little was dead, so he must go on from there.

14

THE town talked of nothing but the shooting. Popular opinion had it that Will Drummond was something of a hero. Nobody had thought he had it in him. What luck he had been in the bank when Marve Little made his break. Fancy a man like Drummond swapping shots with a gunhand like Marve and coming off best. Drummond's hand was shaken, his back slapped. He seemed to blossom modestly under the treatment. Even Penshurst congratulated him on his coolness and presence of mind.

The coroner, a sad-eyed medico of middle years, asked a lot of pertinent questions. Drummond answered like a respectable citizen doing his duty. He wanted no credit, it was a terrible thing to have killed a man, even a man as bad as Marve Little had undoubtedly been. When it came to McAllister's statement, the coroner seemed to hesitate. McAllister dwelled on the curious coincidence of both Darcy and Little being killed by a .38 gun. He pointed out that there was undoubtedly a connection between the killing of Art Malloy, Fred Darcy and Frank Little. Now there was the killing of Marve Little. The coroner seemed to think that the other killings were no concern of his. McAllister dwelled on the strangely timely presence of Drummond in the bank. But it got him nowhere. The coroner's curiosity was aroused, but he ruled that Drummond had killed Marve Little with justification. He even seemed to think that McAllister, having been careless enough to let a prisoner escape, should thank his lucky stars that a good citizen like Drummond had been there to stop the runaway.

Next, McAllister showed his report to the judge. The old man was three-parts drunk, but his brain was working all right. He read the document through, then cocked his head at McAllister.

"By God," he said, "you don't mince

matters, boy. This is practically an accusation of murder against Drummond. But you don't have any evidence. You'll have to do better than this."

"I aim to," McAllister said.

"Find out who that gun belongs to," the judge told him. "And, has it occurred to you that an awful lot of witnesses are now dead?"

"It sure did."

"So you yourself may shortly be a target."

"I reckoned that too."

"I should avoid dark alleyways at night," the judge pronounced.

McAllister grinned.

"I aim to," he said.

He walked to the gunsmith on Garrett and showed him the gun. The man said he had never seen it before. McAllister walked down to the bank and found Drummond in the company of Penshurst.

Drummond looked up from his desk in the inner office and said: "It's customary to knock before you enter a gentleman's office."

McAllister took the gun from his pocket and laid it on the desk.

"Ever see that before?" he demanded.

Drummond shook his head.

"No, I didn't. Should I have?"

McAllister turned to Penshurst who sat at his own desk looking troubled.

"Did you, Mr. Penshurst?"

"I—I don't think so."

McAllister handed it to him. The banker's hands were shaking.

"No," Penshurst said with a look at Drummond. "No—I guess I never saw it before. Mind you, it is not an uncommon weapon. It is possible . . ."

McAllister put the gun in his pocket and said: "Thank you, gentlemen." He walked out.

Penshurst sat looking troubled.

Drummond said: "You look worried. Did you see that gun before?"

"I—no, it's ridiculous. There are so many . . ."

"You don't seem sure."

"It's crazy . . . but . . . well, for a

236

moment I thought it was that pocket pistol of yours."

Drummond smiled easily.

"You were quite right to think that. I did have a gun like that. But it was not the same one. I lost mine a couple of months back as it so happens, but it was not that gun. I looked with particular care. Mine was in a much better condition."

The banker looked relieved.

"That's that settled, then," he said.

Drummond reached for his hat and said: "I think I'm all through here. I'll walk back to my own office." He nodded to Penshurst and walked out. He wanted to be alone, to think. McAllister didn't have a thing to go on, but he was getting close. Too close for comfort.

He went into the Golden Fleece by the side door and went straight into the office. He found his bottle there and took a stiff drink. He was drinking more than usual lately. He found it steadied him up a little and he needed to be steady.

He sat and mused, not pushing his

thoughts, but allowing them to come. The foremost of them was that McAllister must die. And soon, before he got any closer. Drummond's men had either gone or were dead. He would either have to hire a gun or do the job ~~yourself~~ himself if ~~you~~ he could hire a dog to bark for ~~you~~ him. He ran his mind down a list of names.

He came up with Dye Ricketts.

He was the same breed as the Little brothers. He could be hired and he was loyal to his hiring. A man with a reputation both for pride of craft and for skill in it. Ricketts it would be. All he had to do was to check that he was still in town. He stood up. He would do that right away.

Pat O'Doran was feeling good. He was walking now and had proved it by sinking a pint in the Golden Fleece. With that under his belt he walked back to the office, belching happily. There he found Jim Carson sitting on the edge of his cot smoking. McAllister sat behind his desk frowning ferociously.

McAllister was thinking. His whole trouble was that he was in a town and he was trying to track down a man in a town. He was not in the right environment. He could track a man in the wilds over rock as good as an Indian, but here in town he was lost. He needed to be a skilled detective and that was something he was not. All he had gained was to rattle Drummond, but he could no more prove that Drummond was his man than fly. And he knew the man would kill him at the first opportunity.

Carson was saying: "But what do you aim to *do*, Rem? We've had God knows how many men killed and you could be the next."

"I know I could be the next an' most likely am," McAllister told him. "You think I'm enjoyin' it or something'?" He ruminated. "All I can do is wait till he makes his try an' nail him then."

Carson argued: "He hires another man or the man kills you. Either way it don't get you anywhere."

McAllister made a sound of disgust and

reached for his hat. He slapped it onto his head and stalked out. Pat looked after him, worried. He let a few minutes pass, then he rose and picked up the greener.

"What do you think you're doin'?" Carson demanded.

"I'm after takin' a small wee walk," Pat told him.

"You got strong all of a sudden."

"It's a miracle, that's what it is," Pat said and went out onto the street. The whole place was dark except for a light here and there. The front of the Golden Fleece blazed with light further down the street. Pat was tempted to go in there for another drink, but he suppressed the temptation.

McAllister walked warily. He knew that this night could be the night and it wasn't a comfortable feeling. He kept to the shadows and away from the light. He kept his eyes turned away from the lights, too, so they would be better in the darkness. Turning right at the intersection, he walked down Garrett to the Penshurst house. There were quite a few people about still and he thought that there were too many people for it to happen here.

The Penshurst door was opened by the daughter. Her eyes came wide at the sight of him. She didn't like him and he didn't take to being disliked by so beautiful a woman.

"Evenin', ma'am," he said, touching the brim of his hat. "Is your father to home."

She hesitated.

"He's here, but I don't know if he'll see anybody."

"Tell him I've come to see about the gun," he said.

"The gun?"

"He'll know what you're talkin' about."

She left him standing at the door and went into the parlor. Her father was sitting in an armchair reading a paper.

"Who is it, my dear?"

"McAllister, the marshal."

She didn't miss his start of alarm.

"What does he want?"

"He says he's come to see about the gun."

"The gun?"

The man was alarmed and couldn't hide the fact.

"What gun's he talking about?"

"Somebody passed Marve Little a gun before he escaped from jail. He brought it over to the bank this morning and asked Will and I if we could identify it."

"And could you?"

"No. No, we could . . . I . . ."

"What, father?"

"At first I thought it was that pocket Colt of Will's."

"Why, that's ridiculous."

"I know. There are many such guns around. Well, show the marshal in. Let us get it over with."

She looked at her father doubtfully for a moment, then went to ask the marshal in. He seemed huge as he loomed into the small room. He towered over her father and his voice seemed to boom softly. She was conscious of the aggressive maleness of the man and was a little angry with herself because of it. She didn't like the man. He stood for everything she hated.

Her father was nervous. He rose from his chair and shook hands, not knowing what to say, waving a hand for McAllister to sit down.

"Shall I leave you?" Emily asked.

"No," McAllister said. "Please stay, ma'am. You may be able to help."

"Now, marshal," Penshurst said. "What can I . . . how can I help you."

"That gun I showed you at the bank this morning, Mr. Penshurst. You said you'd never seen it before."

"That was true, I had not. Never."

McAllister let that statement hang in the air for a moment.

Finally, he said: "But you hesitated. Why?"

The banker stared at him wordlessly for a moment.

The girl said: "Are you doubting my father's word, sir?"

Penshurst waved her to silence. McAllister said: "What makes you think I doubt his word?"

243

"Your manner."

"I apologise for it. I don't mean to doubt his word, though I may doubt his memory. There's more than one gun of that pattern in this town and I wondered how he could be so sure he hadn't seen that one before."

"I don't think I like——"

Penshurst said: "That's all right, my dear. I can handle this." He turned to McAllister—"As you said, marshal, there are several guns of that kind in town and I wanted to be sure."

"But you weren't sure."

"Not at first."

"Were you sure when I left? Are you sure now?"

"Er—I—reasonably."

"Reasonably isn't good enough, Mr. Penshurst. If you think you've seen this gun before I want you to say so." He took the gun from his pocket and held it up for them to see. Glancing up at the girl he saw the look on her face.

"I—I know a gun like it," the banker said.

McAllister turned to the girl.

"An' you, ma'am," he said. "Do you know a gun like it?"

Her eyes said "yes" but out loud, she said: "No. No, I never saw it before."

McAllister said to the banker: "The gun you know like it, who owns it?"

The banker was white to the lips. He looked at his daughter and didn't find any help there.

"You're putting me in a very embarrassing position, marshal," he said.

"Murder's embarrassing too."

"Murder?"

It was the daughter who spoke.

McAllister said: "Let's see what we have. Fred Darcy tried to leave town. Somebody shot him with a thirty-eight gun."

"There are folks who say that you killed him, marshal," Emily said.

"Emily!" her father protested.

"Sure," McAllister said easily. "That's how it was meant to look. All right, Fred was killed with a thirty-eight. Nothing really unusual in that. Now Marve Little is passed a thirty-eight and he breaks out of jail with it. He's stopped by Will Drummond and killed."

"What are you tryin' to imply?" the girl demanded.

"Why, ma'am," McAllister said innocently, "I ain't tryin' to imply anythin'. I'm just thinking my thoughts out loud like. Aw, yes, there's another fact that's real interestin'. Not long before Fred Darcy got himself shot with this thirty-eight, his saloon was bought from him by a man who once owned a thirty-eight, I'll bet."

"Who?" asked the banker.

"Will Drummond."

"What?" Father and daughter shouted the question together.

"Wasn't it Drummond who you thought owned that thirty-eight, Mr. Penshurst?"

The banker didn't look at him.

"Well, yes. Will did own a gun like that. But that signifies nothing. The purest coincidence I feel sure."

The girl almost screamed: "This is

ridiculous. You've picked on one of the most important men in town . . . you're jealous . . . you came into town without a cent to your name. You're nothing but a gunman and you dare to stand there and—"

"Emily!"

"This man goes around bullying—"

"Emily, you will be silent. Now, Mr. McAllister, Your allegations I'm sure are quite unfounded."

McAllister stood up and towered over them both.

"I'm not makin' any allegations, sir. I'm just stringin' the facts together. They don't add up, but they will. All I want is for you to be sure this isn't the gun Will Drummond owns."

Penshurst waved his hands.

"Will gave a perfectly acceptable explanation, even if it is the same gun. He lost it some time ago. It could be the same gun, but it now has no connection with Will Drummond."

"Now are you satisfied?" the girl demanded.

247

"Ma'am," McAllister said, looking her straight in the eyes, "I shan't be satisfied till I find the man who killed my friend and yours—Art Malloy."

She dropped her eyes; her face was white.

"I'll show you to the door," she said.

When they were at the door, McAllister turned and said: "It don't give me no pleasure, ma'am, that I'm bringin' grief to a woman as beautiful as you."

She laid a hand on his arm.

"You were a real friend of Art's?" she said.

"Yes, ma'am. Only reason I took the badge."

"If you find the man who killed him, I'll be satisfied. I loved him, Mr. McAllister."

"Yes, ma'am. I know that."

"And you suspect Will Drummond, however crazy it may sound," she said in what was almost a whisper.

"Just a hunch," he said. "I'm part Indian, ma'am, an' I run on hunches. They take the place of brains."

248

He turned and walked away.

She stayed where she was staring after him for a moment, her eyes troubled. Her world seemed to be collapsing about her. Could the craziness of this Texas gunfighter be founded on the truth? Was it just possible that the gentle Will Drummond had gunned down Art and Darcy and then cold-blooded planned Marve Little's escape so that he could kill him? It couldn't be. But there was doubt in her mind now and she was honest enough to recognise the fact.

She closed the door and walked back into the parlor.

Her father said: "It can't be possible what the marshal said."

"He didn't say anything, father," the girl told him. "Don't worry. He's only doing his duty and clutching at straws. It'll blow over. We know that Will would never be mixed up in anything criminal."

"No," Penshurst said, "of course, you're right." But she knew that there was doubt in his mind too. The sight of the gun had unnerved him.

"You go on up to bed, father," she said. "I'll read awhile." She sat down and picked up her book. He got to his feet and she thought how old he looked. Placing a hand on her shoulder, he said: "Don't worry, daughter. It'll blow over. Will couldn't possibly be what McAllister suggests he is. A man couldn't fool the pair of us for so long."

She patted his hand.

"Of course not," she said. He bent and kissed her on the forehead. When he had left the room, she sat staring at the page of the book without seeing it. She knew that she couldn't bear to sit still, not while she had so much on her mind, not while her head was so full of unanswered questions. She had to see Will and now. Staying where she was for nearly fifteen minutes, she listened to her father's movements above. Then she fetched a cloak and shawl from her room and let herself out of the rear of her house. She knew that she was sick with fright, but she knew that she must go through with it. She owed it to Art Malloy and to herself.

15

THE woman opened the door. Drummond was at his desk, a drink at his elbow.

"There's a man here," she said in her deep voice. "Says his name's Ricketts."

"Did he come by the rear door?"

"Yes."

"Good. Show him in."

A few minutes later, Ricketts entered. It was the first time Drummond had ever seen him and he looked him over carefully.

In appearance, he was the most unremarkable man possible, the kind who could stand unnoticed in a crowd, a man who mingled without effort with any background. A store clerk, you would say: pale eyes that looked upon the world mildly; a drooping mustache of indeterminate color; a rather weak chin. Drummond looked at his hands and saw that they were white and soft. Ricketts was not a man who favored physical labor; he was a man of skills and he lived by them. He wore a simple suit of brown, the pants pushed into high boots. On his head was a wide-brimmed hat set straight. There was no gun in sight. At once, Drummond feared that he was mistaken in his man.

"Mr. Drummond?"

"Yes. Are you Ricketts?"

"That's correct!" The voice was quiet and hesitant.

"Sit down."

The man in brown sat down primly, well-forward in the chair, knees together like a prim schoolmarm; he put his hands on his knees and sat staring at them.

"Drink?"

"No, thanks. Never touch the stuff."

Drummond poured himself one and offered the man a cigar. Ricketts shook his head—"Thanks, no. I don't smoke." Drummond wanted to ask: "Do you go with women?" but he refrained. He stood looking down at the man, puzzled and a little worried.

"You know why I wanted to see you?'
he asked.

The eyes flicked up at him briefly and
down again.

"Men only want to see me for one
thing, Mr. Drummond. They want a man
killed. That's my job." The same gentle
tone. Drummond came to the conclusion
that the man was stark mad.

"I want a man killed. And I want him
killed quickly."

"Is he here in town?"

"Yes."

"Give me his name and I'll name my
price."

"Price first."

"Very well. My usual charge is five
hundred dollars."

That shook Drummond. He hadn't
thought of anything like that price.

"That's high," he said.

The eyes flicked up and down again.

"How much do you usually pay for a
killing?"

"One fifty on agreement. The same
after the job is done."

"That's not a good craftsman's pay, Mr. Drummond, and I imagine you know it. I'll work for five hundred if it's a normal straightforward killing."

"I'll go to four hundred and no more," Drummond said.

"I haven't made myself sufficiently clear," Ricketts said. "My price is five hundred. I never haggle. If you don't like the price, I suggest you hire yourself another man."

Drummond knew he'd met his match.

"Very well," he said. "I'll pay five hundred."

Ricketts raised his eyes and lowered them again.

"Who's the man?"

"McAllister."

"The marshal?"

"Yes."

The eyes were raised and this time they fixed themselves on Drummond's.

"Mr. Drummond, you haven't been altogether fair to me," the gunman said. "Nobody could call killing McAllister a normal straightforward killing."

"A bullet stops him like it does any other man."

"I know McAllister and I've seen him work. He's liable to shoot back. This will cost you seven hundred."

Drummond ground his teeth together. He was so angry that he could have hit the mild man in brown.

"Are you afraid of being shot at?" he demanded.

The man said with the same mildness: "I'm not afraid of anything, Mr. Drummond. Do you accept the price or not?"

Drummond walked to the other side of the room, knowing the man had him. He had to have McAllister dead and quick. He didn't want to face the man himself.

A tap came at the door.

"Come."

The housekeeper entered, her face heavy and impassive.

"Miss Penshurst is here to see you."

Drummond was startled. What in heaven's name could Emily want this time of night.

"Can't you see I'm busy, woman. I can't see her now."

"I put her in the parlor. You'd best see her."

"She'll have to wait."

"She'll wait."

The woman withdrew, closing the door behind her. Drummond turned to the gunman.

"You'll have to go now. I have a visitor."

Ricketts stood up, his hands at his side, his attitude meek and submissive again.

"Do you want me to do the job?"

"Yes, I suppose so. Yes. But you must do it soon. Is that understood?"

The man nodded.

"I'll do it tonight when he does his rounds. That'll be half in advance."

Drummond protested.

"I don't keep that much money in the house."

"How much do you have?"

"A couple of hundred." He couldn't risk more. McAllister might manage to kill the man and the money would be lost.

"I'll accept that."

Drummond went to his desk, unlocked a drawer and drew out a bundle of notes. He handed them to Ricketts who carefully and laboriously counted them. Satisfied, he thrust them into a pocket. Drummond fumed.

Ricketts said: "The woman who let me in—is she to be trusted?"

"Yes."

"She won't talk?"

"No. Not a chance."

"Right. There's nothing more to be said. I'll have your man dead by dawn. You don't know me. You never spoke to me or saw me before in your life."

"That's understood."

The pale eyes flicked up to Drummond's face for a second and then the man was gone. For a moment, Drummond was overcome by an unusual physical weakness. He leaned against the table and placed a hand on his forehead. If anybody could kill McAllister that cold man would.

He pulled himself together and walked

into the parlor where Emily Penshurst awaited him. She turned toward him as he entered in the room and he knew at once from the expression on her face that something was wrong.

"My darling," he said and opened his arms to her.

She stayed where she was, staring at him. Going up to her, he put an arm around her shoulder and kissed her affectionately on a cheek.

"You look upset," he told her. "Come, tell me and we'll straighten it out."

"McAllister just came to our house," she told him.

He looked surprised, but he didn't show the alarm that arose in him.

"Whatever could he want?"

"He brought that wretched gun."

"What gun?"

"The one he showed you and father today at the bank. The gun that was taken from Marve Little's body. Somebody passed it to him in the jail."

He put a puzzled look on his face. He

held her at arm's length and looked fondly into her face.

"But how can that possibly concern you, my dear?" he asked.

"He brandished that awful gun under our noses and practically accused us of knowing that it was yours."

"Mine? But this is absolutely ridiculous." He folded her into his arms again and hugged her close. "You're not to give it another thought, darling. The gun isn't mine and I think the marshal knows that. He's just desperate to find somebody to accuse for the shootings and doesn't know which way to turn. Go home, forget about it."

"But he hinted . . ."

"What did he hint?"

"That you killed Fred Darcy and arranged for Marve Little to escape so that you could kill him. I'm frightened, Will."

"No need for you to be frightened at all, honey," he told her. "I'm not worried in the slightest. There's nothing to worry about."

"There is, Will."

He showed surprise again.

"How do you mean?"

"That gun was yours."

He fell back from her.

"What?" he whispered.

"The gun was yours," she said determinedly, watching him levelly. "I remember the scratch near the handle."

"You're not making sense," he said. "And even if it was mine, it doesn't mean a thing. I lost it months ago. I told your father."

"You told him today. Not months ago."

"Look, honey, you're overwrought. You're not making sense. What kind of a fool would a man in my position be to commit the killings you're accusing me of?"

"I'm not accusing you of anything, Will. I'm merely saying you lied about the gun."

"Look, just what're you trying to do? You owe me some loyalty."

"I'm trying to find the man who killed Art Malloy."

That was like a slap in the face to him. He stared at her as if he couldn't believe what he was hearing.

"So that old ghost walks again," he said.

"He's walked since he was killed."

He got a grip on himself with an effort. He knew that he must be alone to think. Crazily the thought that he should kill this girl came into his head, but he dismissed it. Not from any softness of heart, but because it would not have been safe to do so.

"Believe me," he said, "the gun was not mine. You're mistaken. I give you my sacred word on that. Now go home and get a good night's sleep and you'll see things differently."

Suddenly, she seemed at a loss. She seemed to look at him one moment as if she were afraid of him, the next as if she despised him.

"Think about what I've said," she told

him. "Think carefully. If you're lying about the gun, I shall find out."

"Emily," he said, "all I know is I love you. We're going to be married and nothing'll stop us. No woman has ever meant as much to me. Remember that. Nothing else matters."

She gave him a long unfathomable look and walked out of the house. He went to the door and watched her as she walked down the street. When he closed the door and turned, he found the housekeeper there.

"I heard every word," she said. "Our time here's getting short."

"Don't you believe it," he said. "We'll stay just as long as I choose."

"Then you'll stay alone."

"What do you mean?"

"They're closing in on us. Get out while the going's good."

"I've got too much tied up in this town."

She snapped: "There's not enough here to hang for," and turned back into her kitchen.

It wasn't true, he thought. He wasn't finished here. There just wasn't enough evidence against him. Good God, there was no evidence at all. Just the gun and that didn't amount to anything. With McAllister dead, everything would be all right.

Ricketts entered a small hotel off Main, mounted to the floor above and tapped four times on a door. It opened and he stepped inside. The man who had let him in closed the door and propped a chair back under the handle. Ricketts sat on one of the two beds in the almost bare room and took off his hat, revealing the fact that he was almost totally bald.

The other man sat on the other bed and said: "Well?"

He was a little man, as nondescript as Ricketts, with watery eyes and a red rose. His hands shook a little and he had a disturbing habit of continually hitching his right shoulder forward as if his coat hung uncomfortably. He was wanted in various States for various crimes among which were child molestation, rape and murder. He had killed two men with a butcher's knife, one with a shotgun and had strangled a woman with a scarf. It gave him pleasure to be paid for committing crimes which to him were a pleasure in themselves. He was not intelligent enough to know pity, but possessed an active animal cunning that had permitted him to live under very trying circumstances. He feared Ricketts whom he regarded as being something of an aristocrat in their gruesome trade.

"He was a little difficult," Ricketts said, "but he saw it my way in the end. There'll be a hundred in this for you, Strip, if you do your part well."

"Bank on it," Strip said. "Who's the party needs killin'?"

Ricketts drew his breath in.

"McAllister," he said.

The watery eyes looked startled for a moment. Then Strip started to giggle.

"Dangerous, killin' a lawman," he said. "But, hell, that bastard needs killin'."

"We do it tonight. Now."

Strip's voice was shrill—
"Now?"
Ricketts nodded. He rose from the bed and started to get ready. He pulled an old and battered case from under the bed and opened it. From it he took a Colt's revolver in beautiful condition, loaded it and stuffed it in the top of his pants. When he had filled a pocket with spare shells which he felt sure he would not need, he took his second weapon from the case. This was a sawnoff shotgun, also in good condition. Meanwhile, Strip also prepared himslf. First, he put on a long overcoat which he left unbuttoned, then he pulled a similar case from under his own bed and from it produced another shortened shotgun. He patted this with affection, loaded it and placed it in a long pocket inside the flap of the overcoat. Ricketts left his shotgun on the bed and donned an overcoat. There was a hole through from the pocket to the inside of the garment. He stuck his hand through this and held the shotgun under cover that way.

The two men grinned at each other wolfishly, pleased with themselves.

"Where's McAllister now?" Strip wanted to know.

"On the streets. All we have to do is to find him."

"Good. Let's go. Christ, I feel good, Dye."

"Me too."

"There jest ain't nothin' like it."

They left their room and went out of the hotel by the side entrance into a dark alleyway.

16

RICKETTS halted outside the Great Western Emporium. He was in deep shadow. Over the way and at an angle to him, a lamp burned outside a saloon. This was the Lively Lady and it was booming. A piano clanged out a tune, voices were raised in raucous disharmony. A man came violently out of the swing doors, staggered across the sidewalk and untied his horse. He leaned against the animal for a moment, then mounted uncertainly. The animal turned slowly, the man raked home the spurs and went careering crazily down the street, giving a wild rebel yell as he went. The few passersby did not turn to watch him go. It was a commonplace to see a shrieking cowhand riding wildly through the streets at the time of night.

A buckboard, drawn by two half-wild mustangs, went quickly down the street.

Strip was on the other side of the street, caught by the lamplight.

Ricketts drifted across the street, got near Strip and said: "Use the shadows, you dumb fool."

Strip muttered something and moved to an alleyway. Ricketts drifted back across the street, went slowly down the sidewalk until he reached the alleyway at the side of a hotel. Here was a large water barrel. He got behind it. He did not have a complete view of the street from here, but he had enough and it was safe. Ricketts was no coward, but he liked to be safe. If McAllister passed now they could catch him in a murderous cross-fire.

A man and woman passed, talking in low voices.

A big man left the sidewalk at the entrance of the alley, crossed it and mounted the sidewalk on the other side. He carried either a rifle or a shotgun and Ricketts knew that this was the big Irish deputy. The gunman didn't like this, but he reckoned that McAllister and O'Doran would not be patrolling the same place at the same time. He worried a little that McAllister had returned to the office. Ricketts toyed with the idea of going to the office and catching him there. He put off making a decision. He'd give the marshal another hour. If he did not come by then, he would head for the office.

As he waited, the people on the street grew less, though the noise from the saloon seemed to increase. The Golden Fleece was to his right and over the way at an angle to him was the Lively Lady. He reckoned that McAllister would be checking on both saloons before the night was done.

After he had stayed still for something like thirty minutes, he heard the shrill sound of a dog. Anybody else than Ricketts hearing it would think the animal had been kicked, but Ricketts knew it for Strip's favorite signal. Their man was coming. Ricketts edged out from his deep shadow and peered up the street. Nothing moved. He glanced across at the Lively

Lady and saw a tall man standing silhouetted against the light of the large window. This he knew to be McAllister.

He took the sawn-off shotgun from under the skirt of his overcoat and placed a thumb and he prayed that his target would move in his direction.

McAllister stayed still for some time, then moved toward the center of the street. Ricketts licked his dry lips. McAllister changed direction and started walking directly toward him. Ricketts slipped back into the shadows, cocking the weapon as he did so. The lawman would cross the mouth of the alleyway and Ricketts would let him have both barrels at close range. The shot should cut him in half. A good clean job and nobody could be in doubt as to its result. You wouldn't have to check if McAllister was dead. He'd be deader than last week's mutton. Strip would fire from the other side of the street. Ricketts had never been surer of himself. This was the kind of neat job he liked to do. He planned to fire and hightail it down the alleyway and straight back to his hotel room. Nobody would be the wiser.

McAllister was thirty yards away and coming on steadily.

McAllister halted.

The street was without movement. The noise of the two saloons almost deafened him.

He thought: *The time and the place to cut down on me.* He had thought the same thought a dozen times during his patrol of the town and he knew he might well think it another dozen times before he was through.

He hefted the greener and went on.

There was an alleyway to his right; another to his left. He could be in a crossfire. His eyes flicked left and right, catching no telltale glimmer of light on metal. But his nerves were taut.

Suddenly a stentorian bellow—
"Down, Rem."

He reacted immediately. The shout was Pat O'Doran's. He hurled himself to the right, struck on his shoulder, somersaulted, stretched out in the dust with the shotgun cocked.

From near at hand a shotgun roared twice, one shot coming so close on the tail of the other that there was one deafening sound.

A man screamed piercingly.

All these sounds were from his right. Somebody had tried to cut down on him from that direction and Pat had let him have both barrels.

Therefore, there could danger to the left.

McAllister swung the shotgun as another weapon roared. This time from the alleyway to his left. Something ripped across his head, burned his back, tore into his shoulders. The flash came from the alleyway. He let go with both barrels. He heard the shot ripping into the woodwork of the building beyond. He rolled desperately, knowing if the man in there lived, there was another barrel to come.

It came and this time it missed.

McAllister reared to his feet, wondering how badly he was hit. But for the moment, it didn't matter; he was moving, staying on his feet. He ran up the street for twenty yards, turned at a right-angle and hit the sidewalk, throwing himself flat.

Pat had reloaded and was firing into the alley.

McAllister got to his feet again and ran forward on the tips of his toes.

Pat shouted: "The bastard's still in there, Rem."

McAllister sweated. He thought of rushing the alleyway, but turned the idea down. Running into two barrels of buck-shot was beyond the call of duty in his opinion.

He looked around him. There were lights burning in the building to his right; an office of some kind. He tried the door and it resisted him. He backed up, hurled himself forward and nearly tore the door from its hinges.

He came face to face with a terrified man who held a gun in his hand. The hand shook violently. The sight of it terrified McAllister.

"I'm the law," he said, "put that fool gun away."

The man swallowed hard and continued to wave the gun around.

McAllister demanded: "Is there another way out of here?"

"Side door into the alley," the man whispered.

McAllister pushed him aside and went through the doorway behind the man. This was an inner office with a large safe in the corner. A door on the other side of the room. McAllister opened this and found himself in a kind of lobby. To his left was a door. It was bolted. He drew the bolts as quietly as he could, paused a moment, filled his lungs with air then wretched the door open. Hurling himself through it, he landed in the alleyway in a long dive, rolled and came up against the building opposite.

A gun thundered.

Something struck the wall above his head. He rolled again, dropped the shotgun which he realised in a moment of panic was empty and drew the Remington.

He could see nothing.

He prayed that Pat didn't start shooting into the alley.

Another shot came. This one was closer, but it showed McAllister the man's position. He fired.

Silence.

He waited.

The man was some twenty feet further down the alley and McAllister reckoned that any minute now he'd run. He was most likely flat on the ground hard up against the opposite wall. If he ran, he would be on his feet faintly silhouetted against the night sky at the end of the alley.

Five minutes passed.

If the other man was alive, he was wondering if McAllister was dead. McAllister was wondering if he had hit the man.

His eyes were becoming more used to the darkness now.

Suddenly, he became aware that there

was a blurred shape against the night sky. The man was walking slowly backward.

McAllister raised the Remington, cocked and fired. A shot racketed back in reply. Blinded by his own gunflash, McAllister rolled to the other side of the alley. Footsteps were pounding away from him. He fired his gun empty. The footsteps continued, the man reached the end of the alley and turned left.

Pumping empty shells out and thumbing fresh loads into the Remington, McAllister shouted: "The next alley east, Pat." His gun loaded, even under the hammer, he ran down the alley. He swung left and a shot winged past his head. He turned right, dropped and found himself amongst the trash of the backlot. He had come to rest in more comfortable places in his life.

He eyed around for the man he was after and couldn't see him. The scene was lit by nothing but the stars.

Reaching around, he found a can with his left hand and hurled it foward as far as he could. A gun sounded from the rear of a building, a good forty paces away and he fired at the flash without much hope of getting a hit. A window collapsed under the shot and he cursed, knowing he would have to be careful else some innocent would get hurt.

Suddenly, the man was on the move again; McAllister heaved himself to his feet and ran too. The man flung a shot back at him, but it was wide. McAllister ran on. After a dozen paces or so, he knew that he was on dangerous ground, for he could not hear the man above the sound of his footfalls and knew the fellow could have stopped.

In the next second, he knew he had made a mistake. A shot came, something struck him hard high in the left arm and he was spun around as he ran. He tripped and fell, lost his gun and had another shot sent at him.

He lay cursing and searching around for his gun.

The man was running again now.

McAllister found his gun, floundered to his feet and found that his left arm felt numb and heavy. But he started running. Ahead was the dark maw of an alley. The dim figure of the man ahead of him disappeared into this. Was Pat in his position at the other end?

McAllister halted, pressed back against the wall and saw the man. From the other end of the alley a man cried out a challenge. In the alley, the man fired. Pat poured fire into the dark way. Lead sang past McAllister. He yelled for Pat to hold his fire. The man was still on the move. A door opened, allowing a shaft of light into the dark alley. For a brief second the man was outlined against it. McAllister lifted his gun, but was afraid of hitting Pat. The door slammed and the light was gone. McAllister started running. He weaved badly and once crashed against the side of the alley and knew that he was in shock from the bullet in his upper arm. He reached the door and tore it open. Knowing that he was a damn fool even as he did it. He charged clean through into a lighted passageway. No shot came. He ran forward and came to the lobby; to his right were the stairs, facing away from him to the street door. The place was deserted.

Had his quarry gone up the stairs or straight through the door ahead of him out onto the street? He had to make a guess and if he was wrong it could cost him his life.

Had Pat seen the man going in through the door? The chances were that he had. Therefore if the man had gone out onto the street Pat would have fired on him. The man must have either gone up the stairs or through the doorway to the left. So had the man taken to that room because it was near to escape or had he gained height by mounting the stairs?

McAllister decided to bet on the stairs.

Edging forward, he craned his neck to see up the stairs, gun cocked, ready for action. A floorboard creaked. He knew from the sounds in the background that there were plenty of men out on the street come to watch the excitement.

In the house, silence pressed down on him. The only sound seemed to be that of his own breathing and his stealthy advance.

He reached the side of the stairs, still craning his neck, yet shifting his gaze every now and then to the door to his left. It was closed tight.

He reached the foot of the stairs, turning, facing upward.

Suddenly, a sound . . . a gun cocking.

The top of a man's head came into view . . . a gun.

They both fired in the same instant, both nervous, both hurried. Wood splintered near him, he hurled himself forward flat against the stairs, gun still forward. The man had disappeared from view. McAllister gathered his right leg under him in preparation of an upward charge. There was no profit in lying where he was, waiting to be shot at. He might as well risk being shot while he went in to finish his adversary.

Hurried movement overhead.

McAllister looked right and glimpsed the man running along the landing. He snapped an awkward sideways shot and knew he'd missed. Getting his feet under him, he pounded up the stairs, reached the top, turned and faced a window with the lights of the street beyond. In that second, he knew he'd been suckered. The man had him in the light, while he himself was below the level of the window in darkness. McAllister fired two shots low. He thought he heard a grunt, but he was moving too fast to know for sure. Leaping forward, he bounded into the air and came down hard on the man with both feet. The air went out of him noisily. McAllister lost his balance and went down. Something clipped him sharply on the side of the head and he fell aginst the wall.

Sound told him that the man was scrambling to his feet. McAllister triggered and found his gun was empty. The man fired at point blank range and missed. His bulk showed briefly against the light. McAllister rose and drove his head into the fellow's belly, his superior weight driving the man backward. With a rending crash the window gave. His adversary went on backward out of the window. He hit the cover of the sidewalk, rolled and disappeared into the street. A shout went up from the crowd down there.

McAllister leaned against the wall and gulped breath into tortured lungs. He was shaking and he wanted to retch. Somebody was yelling up from the street, wanting to know if he was alive. Most likely Pat.

The street door slammed back and boots sounded below. Doors opened on the landing and heads appeared. McAllister started emptying his gun of used shells and thumbing fresh rounds in. It gave him something to do while he recovered himself.

Boots sounded on the stairs. In a moment, Pat appeared, his face concerned.

"You all right, boy?"

"I'm all right, Pat. Took some lead in the arm is all." Pat's powerful arm was around him and he shook it off. He could manage. He walked downstairs on rubbery legs and was glad to get out in the cool night air. The man he had chased into the house lay on the edge of the street, his head at an awkward angle. His face showed in the lamplight and it was not pretty; the eyes stared straight ahead, the lips were drawn back in a snarl. He wore a long overcoat.

"Anybody know him?" McAllister asked.

"Sure," Pat said, "that's Ricketts."

"A killer," another man added.

"The other one?"

"Dead. Up the street a piece. Hung around with Ricketts. No-account and deadly."

McAllister put his hand on Pat's arm.

"You saved my life, I reckon. Thanks."

"Any time," said Pat.

McAllister went through the man's pockets and found nothing of consequence except for a roll of money. It was a lot of money for a man of this kind to be carrying. McAllister handed it to Pat and started for the office. He heard Pat say: "Somebody get the doc."

On the way to the office, he felt like fainting, but he didn't because only women were allowed to do that. Ten minutes later, the doctor saw to his wound in the arm. The bullet, he pronounced, had done no more than cut the flesh. It would hurt a bit and he had lost too much blood, but he'd be all right. The next hour was spent in digging buckshot out of him, his shoulders and his back. The shot had torn his scalp in a couple of places. The doctor said he'd been lucky it had missed his eyes. Then the doctor left and the three lawmen sat there drinking whiskey.

The door opened.

Three guns were directed at it.

Emily Penshurst came into view. They put their guns away and McAllister grinned.

"Nearly got yourself shot, ma'am," he said. "We're all of us a little jumpy after just now."

"I heard you were shot, Mr. McAllister."

"Just a mite."

"It isn't serious?"

"No, ma'am."

"I—I'm sorry. I hope you'll take care. Don't expose yourself on the street any more."

"No, ma'am," he said gravely. "I'll keep myself well-hidden."

"Now, you're mocking me."

"God forbid."

"What I mean is . . . we have lost one . . . good law officer in this town we don't want to lose another."

McAllister stood up. His arm was in a sling and his head was bandaged so that he felt like a hero of a melodrama.

"That's a fine sentiment, ma'am, one I can second," he said.

"That's all I wanted to say. Now I'll go."

McAllister reached for his hat and put it on.

"I'd admire to walk you home, Miss Emily," he told her.

286

"No, thank you. You should stay here. I'll be safe enough."

"Can't allow it," said McAllister. "These streets ain't no place for a lady at night."

"You're crazy to go out after what happened," Carson said.

McAllister smiled. "The man tryin' to kill me is right out of killers right now."

Pat said: "I'll go."

McAllister said: "You're just tryin' to spoil my pitch, boys. It ain't often a homely Texas cow nurse like me gets to escortin' an elegant lady like Miss Penshurst an' I don't aim to miss out on it."

She blushed and smiled.

Given time, McAllister thought, *we could mean something to each other.* It was a nice thought and it pleased him.

Out on the sidewalk, he offered her his injured arm and she took it gently. There were still people about and they eyed the pair curiously. Emily behaved as if they weren't there.

They paced unhurriedly down Main

and turned down Garrett. It was a fine starlit night. It was hard to believe with this sweet-smelling silent woman at his side that so short a while before two men had tried to murder him and they had both died. A sudden gratitude for being alive at all came to him. Having Emily Penshurst with him was a kind of bonus that he hadn't expected.

He started thinking about Will Drummond. He would like to see the man's face when he heard that McAllister had escorted his girl home. Then the thought hit him that the woman could be a decoy. She could be leading him straight into another bullet.

Looking down at the delicate profile below him, he discredited the suspicion.

She must have become conscious of his gaze, for she turned her head and raised her eyes to him. He thought that he had never seen a finer pair in his life. She smiled and he patted the hand on his arm.

"What were you thinking, Mr. McAllister?" she asked.

"I was thinking you could be leading

me into a trap," he said gently. "He's tried everythin' else. A woman as lovely as you might clinch it for him."

She didn't get mad at him, which surprised him.

In a low voice, she said: "Who has tried everything else?"

"Drummond," he said.

There was silence between them for a moment. Then she halted and turned to him.

"Should you make wild accusations like that in your position?" she asked.

"You'll see," he said.

"I thought perhaps . . . I didn't like you at first . . . I thought you coarse and hard." She stopped, drew a breath and went on. "Then I thought . . . well, I changed my mind somewhat. Now I hear you saying things like that about a fine man . . ."

He smiled.

"Just put it down to crazy jealousy," he said.

"How can you joke?" she said.

"I said it lightly," he said. "I ain't

jokin'. I'm deadly serious. If Drummond was out of the way, I might stand a chance."

She didn't know what to do. She felt a little mad, but at that moment she didn't want to be mad with him. Somehow she liked walking quietly through the starlight with this big self-assured man.

"The trouble with you, Mr. McAllister," she said, "is you don't know the rules."

"One thing my ol' daddy taught me with a belt buckle, Miss Emily," he told her, "was that when courtin' a lady or fightin'—there ain't no rules. You're out to win or you didn't ought to start in."

"I should be angry with you."

"Later. Get mad at me when the stars go in an' your pa asks you where you were this time of night."

She laughed.

"He's asleep. All the gun shots in the world wouldn't wake him once he's asleep."

They strolled on and came to her home. "I have been complimented on my coffee," she said. "May I offer you a cup."

A trap, his mind told him. *It has to be a trap. This is too easy.* Then he looked at the girl again and told himself he was a fool.

"I'd like that," he said. "But won't folks talk."

She looked up at him and laughed.

"You *are* old-fashioned, Mr. McAllister," she said.

She led the way around the side of the house, let him into the kitchen and turned up the lamp on the table. She told him to sit down. He found a chair which gave him a view of the outside door and the door leading into the house. She put the pot on the stove. They talked. He told her something of his life, about his old man and about his not knowing whether his mother had been Mexican or Cheyenne, remarking that his father had told so many stories she could have been a Vermont Sunday school teacher, for all he knew. But that was something that didn't matter—a man was what he was and that was the end of it.

He told her of his boyhood, the hardness of it, how he never knew whether he would be living with his father or boarded out with some ranching family or other, how twice he had lived with the Cheyenne.

"My," she said, "you must have had an unhappy childhood."

"Unhappy!" he exclaimed amazed. "Why, ma'am, I had the happiest childhood a man ever could have." There had always been something to learn, to do. He had never been still from one minute to another. He had learned to hunt, ride the wild ones, learned to track like an Indian, to talk Cheyenne and Spanish, he had learned cow-sense, he had . . . why he had once even learned to read. He'd been scared and hungry, but he could never remember being really unhappy. The world was a good place to live in and if you gave the human race a chance on its own terms it was made up of a pretty good set of people. Sure there were some bad ones, but that was what guns were for.

"You make it all so simple," she said. "Don't you ever find yourself puzzled by life?"

"No, ma'am," he told her. "Puzzlement is for the smart fellers. I ain't smart, I'm just cunnin' like an animal or an Indian. I keep alive, I have fun and I reckon that's enough for any man."

"I wish I had your confidence."

"You're a beautiful woman, you don't need it. All you need is a man who has it."

The coffee boiled over. She jumped up with a cry, covered her hand with a cloth and whisked it to the table. She poured and they sat sipping coffee.

"Emily," he said suddenly, "I want you to know I wish it didn't have to be this way."

"What do you mean?"

"Drummond."

She looked away from him, trying to hide her face from his searching eyes.

"You do not have any proof," she said.

293

"It does you credit that you want to find Art's murderer, but this isn't the way to find him. Will Drummond is well-thought of in this town. I respect him and I hope to marry him."

McAllister said: "You suspect as much as I do, so you might as well face up to it now. You won't marry Drummond while I'm alive. That's for sure."

She turned and looked at him.

"You have absolutely nothing to go on," she said.

"I soon shall have."

"How?"

"Because it's my guess he's used every way he can think of killing me an' he's about run out of killers. He'll have to do it himself."

"You can't mean this. You just can't."

"I can and I do. Break it off with him, girl. Now. There'll only be grief in it for you."

She started to cry. McAllister was distressed; he hated women crying. He never knew what to do.

"Now, see here, ma'am . . ." He rose. "Aw, shucks . . ."

He put a hand on her shoulder, she laid a wet cheek against his hand. Putting a hand under her chin, he lifted her face a little so that she looked at him. He could think of only one thing to do and that was to kiss her, mostly because he wanted to. So he kissed her. In the first moment, her mouth trembled under his. He put on a little pressure and slowly she responded. He lifted her to her feet, their mouths still locked and suddenly, she clung to him. They strained at each other, not able to get close enough.

When at last he took his mouth from hers, he found that he was trembling slightly. It was rather a pleasant sensation.

She said: "You'll think I'm a bad woman."

"If I did, it would be mighty ungrateful. I think you're the most wonderful woman I ever did see."

She smiled wanly.

"You know the right words," she said.

"I know the right actions too," he told her and lowered his mouth to hers again. She was thinking of Will Drummond. Here, right in this house, he had made love to her. Maybe at heart she was a bad woman. Suddenly, she didn't care. McAllister was right, he had the confidence for both of them. She was in his hands. She couldn't remember when she had felt happier.

At last, she managed to say: "I think you should go."

He stepped back from her, smiling down at her flushed face, and saying: "I'll go if you want me to."

"You know I don't want you to."

He grinned boyishly.

"Then I won't go. I reckon we're old enough to make up our own minds what we want to do."

She came into his arms with a rush. She hurt his wounded arm, but he didn't care much.

17

AN hour later, he kissed her at the door. The lamp was dim and her dark hair had fallen about her face. She looked very beautiful.

She said: "We haven't decided anything. Now I have another problem in place of my old one."

"You have no problem with me, honey," he said. "I gave it you straight. I ain't marrying right now, but I love you like hell. I ain't promisin' nothin'. We have what we have and let's make the best of it. Your problem with Drummond is easily solved. Cut adrift, fast. Tomorrow. See him and tell him."

"But there's my father. He depends on Will."

"Drummond won't be there to depend on when I take him."

"You know," she said, "when I'm with you, nothing seems to matter much."

"That's the way it should be." He kissed her and patted her on the bottom. She clung to him for a moment and whispered: "Please be careful."

"I always am."

He stepped out into the night and she closed the door softly behind him. He stood for a moment, getting his eyes used to the dim light of the stars, thinking, glad that Emily Penshurst had not been a trap. He liked her and she sure made sweet love. He wished she could be let down lightly over Drummond, but she could not. There was not much of a future ahead of her unless she met a good and steady man. But that was the way it went. What had to be done, had to be done.

He walked around the house.

At once he saw that there was a man standing under the cottonwood tree beyond the picket fence. He didn't stop, but his hand slipped down onto the butt of the Remington. As he came through the gateway, the man stepped forward.

"McAllister—a word."

It was Drummond.

"Yes."

He couldn't see the man's face, for it was hidden under the brim of the hat, but he knew from every line of the man's body that he was held in the grip of tension and rage.

"I saw you."

"So?"

"You've been in there with the woman I intend to marry."

McAllister laughed.

"You ain't marryin' anybody, Drummond," he said. "You're goin' to hang by that fancy neck of yourn."

"Stop that foolishness. You know perfectly well that I am a respectable and law abiding citizen. You don't have an atom of proof against me. If you don't stop spreading that story I shall bring a case in law against you."

"Go ahead and see where it gets you."

"You'll leave that girl alone or I—I'll—"

"You'll what?"

"I'll kill you."

McAllister said: "You tried that often enough already without no success. Try it now, Drummond."

They eyed each other.

Drummond stood consumed by rage, his hands clenching and unclenching.

McAllister stepped up close to him and repeated: "Try it now, you yeller-livered coyote."

Drummond stepped a pace backward.

"You're a braggart and a bully, McAllister. You know I'm no hand with a gun."

"I know you're a murderous skunk, Drummond. All you have the guts for is shooting men in the back. Like you shot Fred Darcy. Or cuttin' 'em down in the dark like Marve Little. Or having other men do it like you had Frank Little done in. Or hiring a couple of gunnies like the two we settled out on the street tonight. Try it now, you yeller bastard."

McAllister hit him with the back of his hand across the face and knocked him from his feet. Maybe this was the moment when he took Drummond. His right hand brushed the handle of the Remington. He prayed the man would produce a gun from somewhere.

Drummond lay where he had fallen. His hat had come up and his face was revealed. His hair had fallen over the eyes that stared at McAllister with crazy intensity. He wiped his mouth with his hand and got slowly to his feet.

"I'll kill you for this, McAllister."

"Do it now."

"I'll choose the time and the place."

"Like you always do," McAllister said. He hit the man again, knocking him back against the tree. He heard the wind go out of him.

The man screamed something at him.

McAllister watched him, thinking that he had never wanted a man dead so much before.

Drummond heaved himself away from the tree, picked up his fallen hat and straightened his clothes. He gave the big man a look of pure hatred and walked off down the street.

McAllister sucked his knuckles meditatively and followed slowly. He reckoned Drummond would make his try soon. His pride wouldn't let him leave it for long.

Drummond entered the house by the kitchen door and the woman looked up at him from her knitting. Her eyes widened as she took in his battered face.

"What happened to you?" she demanded.

"Shut your ugly mouth," he told her and walked past her into the house.

She laid down her knitting and thought a while. She knew the signs. Drummond was starting to crack. What they had working for them here was about to fall apart. When it did, she wouldn't be here. She was one to look after herself.

When McAllister walked into the office, the lamp was low and Pat and Carson were asleep. He felt his way to the desk and found the whiskey. He had taken his second mouthful when Carson woke up. He reached over and turned up the light.

After a good look at McAllister he said:

"You look like the cat that got the cream."

McAllister smiled gently.

"I got the cream tonight," he said enigmatically, "but tomorrow I get best prime streak."

"What the hell's that supposed to mean?" Carson demanded.

"It means I got right under Drummond's skin and pretty soon he's comin' for me in person."

"Don't you ever give up?" Carson said. "You still don't have a damned thing on the man."

"Tonight he threatened to kill me. What more do you want than that?"

"What did you have to do to get him to say that?"

"That'd be tellin'. Have a drink."

"No, thank you. I'd druther have my sleep."

"Every man to his taste."

The following day was one of inaction and anti-climax, yet at the same time, because of both, it was a day of tension. Jim

Carson steadily maintained that McAllister was mistaken and that Drummond was an innocent citizen. Pat was made of simpler stuff. McAllister was anxious and McAllister wasn't a man to be that way about nothing, therefore it added that there must be something to be anxious about. Maybe Drummond was innocent, but you couldn't be too sure when it came to staying alive, so he reckoned that, like McAllister, he would regard the man as guilty until he was proven innocent. So when McAllister patrolled through the town, Pat drifted along somewhere in the rear. Neither made comment on the fact.

McAllister reckoned he was safe enough during daylight hours. The danger would come when he patrolled the town after dark.

"For the love of God, boyo," Pat said, "leave the night patrol to me. Nobody wants me dead. Stay in the office and keep Jim company."

McAllister snarled: "I ain't skulking in the office for nobody." Which seemed to settle it. Pat grumbled and reconciled himself to getting little sleep. McAllister prowled around town trying to think of a way to provoke Drummond into showing his hand, preferably in public. Once he met the man on the street outside the Golden Fleece. He greeted the man with cheerful insolence, but Drummond ignored him. At another time, he came face to face with Emily Penshurst and her father. He touched his hat politely and offered her a small bow. The banker nodded in a not too friendly manner. The girl bowed her head and flashed him a warm smile.

As they passed out of earshot, Penshurst said: "That man makes me uneasy. I shall be glad when Carson is fit again and he can move on."

"Maybe he'll stay, father," she said.

"Not him," he told her, "he's not the staying kind."

His daughter was silent till they reached the store and she left him. He passed on to the bank, thinking that Emily had an exceptionally fine color this morning and her eyes were unusually bright.

McAllister leaned up against a sidewalk upright and thought about last night. Pity he wasn't a settling man. Emily Penshurst would be a mighty fine woman to settle with. He sighed and went on his way.

The day dragged on. He ate his mid-day meal with Pat in the eating-place, took Jim Carson's meal to him and then slept the afternoon through while Pat kept an eye on the town. He awoke at five in the evening, washed up and had a shave at the pump to the rear of the office, sat talking with Jim Carson for a while and then strolled through the town. A small bunch of trail-drivers came rocketing in from the grazing grounds, he greeted them and reminded them to park their guns. They all knew him and were civil enough. He paid the red-light district a visit, had a beer with a leading madam, then walked back to Garrett. Here he met Emily again. She blushed at the sight of him and he was glad that she was alone.

"Emily," he said, "I've been thinkin' about last night—"

She looked at his feet and said: "Don't dare remind me of it, sir." There was no reproach but only warmth in her voice.

"I've been remindin' me of it all day, I reckon. I'll be rememberin' it till I'm an old man."

"You and your Texas soft tongue."

"It's God's truth."

"Rem," she said, "father said you'll be moving on when Mr. Carson's well again. Is that so?"

"I never tried to fool you, girl."

"I know. You're honest at least."

"Least!" he snorted. "Bein' honest ain't least. It's the most. Say, Emily, could we walk this evening. I ain't never seen you in the moonlight."

She laughed.

"Can you guarantee a moon?"

"It'll be there."

"Then I can't refuse."

"Good. When and where?"

"Out back of my place at nine?"

"Sure. Pat can have the town for a while."

She gave him a smile and went on her way. Her thoughts were confused. She no longer knew where she stood with Will Drummond and she was almost sure that McAllister was right and Drummond had been mixed with the killings. She realised that she had nothing to go on and that it was McAllister's strength of character that had convinced her. Now she didn't seem to care. For the first time in her life only today seemed to matter. Why did that man McAllister so easily convince her that being herself was right? Maybe she would regret this bitterly later. But somehow she was sure that she would not. McAllister could ride away tomorrow and she would remember him only in a warm and even grateful way. There was nothing mean and small about the man, he didn't pretend to be something he was not. He admitted to being what he was. He didn't want to settle, so he would not. If she had refused him, he would have walked away with regret but without malice.

She found herself singing as she went into the house.

McAllister was humming to himself as he went into the office. Pat smoked his pipe behind the desk. Carson was cutting his nails with his pocket knife.

Carson snarled: "All right for you to look so damned happy. You ain't chained to this Goddam bed."

McAllister played a game of checkers with him and that seemed to cheer him a bit. Then McAllister carefully dismantled and cleaned his gun, washed his hands, combed his hair and said: "Pat, keep an eye on the town for a while, will you?"

The Irishman said: "Sure. Holy saints, if I didn't know better, I'd say you was after courtin' a wee girl."

"Would you now," said McAllister, slipped into his coat and went out onto the street. Dusk was dropping softly over the town. He walked a block, halted at the mouth of the alleyway there, spent five minutes watching the street, then slipped into the alley. Reaching the end, he turned half-left and crossed an empty lot. He walked until he had the Penshurst place on his left and some trees on his right, then swung into the trees. It was almost pitch dark under there. He waited patiently for thirty minutes, not seeing any movement to rouse his suspicion, till the kitchen door of the house opened and the figure of the girl was briefly silhouetted against the light. He went foward to meet her and a moment later she was in his arms. They kissed, then went arm in arm through the trees.

"This," she said, "is as crazy as can be, but I'm happy. Are you happy, Rem?"

He said: "I feel so durned good I could sing and dance." He put his arm around her and she slipped her own around his waist.

Slowly, they went through the timber toward the creek. She thought: *If only I weren't a woman and I could ride away with this man.* Go and see far places, get out of the rut of being a woman in a man's world. Yet that was plain foolishness, because she had never been more glad that she was a woman.

They stopped near the creek, he took off his coat and they lay down on it together, talking softly, foolishly and greatly to their pleasure. They stayed there for an hour and during all that time Emily never wondered once how she, a lady, came to be lying on the ground by a creek with a man as rough as this. If she had thought of such a thing a short time before she would have been deeply shocked. After an hour, she sat up, arranged her hair and said, smilingly: "You do muss a woman, so, sir."

He kissed her and she put her arms around his neck.

"Enough of that," he said, "I have to get you home. Where're you supposed to be at, by the way?"

"At a girl friend's."

He strapped on his gun and stood. She rose and took his hand. Suddenly, he stiffened. Startled, she looked around. He was staring toward the timber, but she could neither hear nor see a thing.

He moved with such sudden violence that she screamed. She was knocked from her feet as the shot came. She fell on the ground screaming. McAllister drew his gun fast and fired two himself down. A shadow flitted in the trees; he fired another shot. Twigs crackled under fleeing feet. He fired again, but knew that he had lost his man. Ejecting spent shells and thumbing in fresh, he rose to his feet.

"Rem."

In a second he was down on one knee at her side.

God, she'd been hit.

Panic swooped through him.

He could see the dark stain on her dress, high up above the heart. The left shoulder. Holstering his gun, he hastily ripped some cloth from the tail of his shirt, rolled it into a tight wad and pressed it down on the wound after he had ripped her dress clear of it.

"Hold that tight against the wound," he ordered her curtly. Her great eyes watched him. He ripped the bandanna from around his neck and tied it around her shoulder. It tended to pull the wadding away from the wound, so he took a length of peggin string that he was never without from his pocket and lashed it around the upper part of her body, pulling the wadding back into place.

"You're goin' to be all right, honey," he said. "No call to be scared now."

"I'm not scared, but I think I'm going to faint."

"Go right ahead. When you wake up the doc'll be looking after you."

He kissed her on the forehead, draped the coat around her and lifted her from the ground. He went along the creekside trail, not risking going into the trees for the short-cut in case the gunman should still be there waiting for them. It took him a good ten minutes to reach Main and he sweated all the way terrified that the girl would die. This was all his damn-fool fault. He was spotted at once and soon he had a crowd around him. Pat came out of the office. A kid was sent scurrying for the doctor. By the time McAllister reached Garrett there must have been more than a hundred people around him. A man being shot wouldn't arouse comment, but a girl like Emily Penshurst getting hit was sure news. Questions were fired at him, but he turned them away. When they knocked at the Penshurst door, the banker answered and he went to pieces at once. McAllister told Pat to clear the crowd away and carried Emily upstairs. He found her room, laid her on the bed lighted the lamp. She opened her eyes and smiled.

He sat on the bed and held her hand.

Penshurst came in and fluttered around, saying that he loved his daughter and please God don't let her die. Emily told him that she had no intention of dying. McAllister suggested Penshurst go and get himself and McAllister a drink. The man weaved off, but he was back in a moment with the doctor.

The young man's face was grave as he bent over Emily and took the dressing off her. He gave the wound a careful inspection and asked McAllister: "Any exit hole in the back?"

"No, the lead's still in there."

The girl looked at McAllister and her eyes pled with him.

The doctor said: "Boiling water."

McAllister went downstairs and found water on the stove. He poured this into a clean bowl and took it upstairs. The doctor poured some carbolic into the water and started cleaning the wound. McAllister had seen some pretty gruesome sights in his life and thought that nothing could affect him, but the sight of the doctor probing the livid wound in the soft white flesh of the girl upset him. Penshurst hurried from the room. McAllister could have used a drink, but he stayed where he was holding the girl's hand. It seemed an eternity before the doctor held up the forceps and showed him the piece of lead.

"Thank God for that," McAllister said.

The doctor dressed the wound with clean wad and bandage.

"Keep her warm and watch for a temperature," the doctor told him. "She'll pull through. She's young and she's strong. I'll look in again at daybreak."

McAllister said: "I have my job, doc—can you send a woman?"

"Sure, I'll get one along right now." The doctor went. Penshurst wandered in with a bottle of whiskey in his hand.

"How is she?" he asked.

"I'm all right, papa," the girl told him. "The doctor says I'm going to be all right."

McAllister took the whiskey from him and drank from the bottle. That made him feel a little better. Penshurst wandered away again. The last half-hour seemed to have aged him ten years.

McAllister sat with the girl until the woman arrived, somebody Emily knew. He patted the white hand that lay on the coverlet and said: "I have a little business to attend to. I'll be right back."

"Be careful."

He grinned reassurance and went downstairs.

Outside, the cool air hit him. Until now he hadn't realised how hot it had been in the house. He thought about what he would do next. His first idea was to get Pat with his shotgun, but he ruled that out. This was personal as well as official. He had to do this himself without help.

So where did he start?

Drummond's place. He'd search the whole town if necessary.

He wondered what frame of mind the man would be in now. Either he could be planning to bluff it out or he could be panicking and ready to run. McAllister thought he was ready to run. In Drummond's boots, he knew *he* would have been.

He started down Garrett.

Will Drummond was confused. For once that brain of his was refusing to remain cool. Ever since he had seen McAllister with the girl he had lost his sense. For the first time in his adult life he had acted on impulse. One man's life had stood between himself and safety and now he had given himself away and that man was hunting him. He had followed McAllister and the girl because he was jealous when he should have been following them because the man had to be killed. The only weapon he had taken with him with a hand-gun when he should have taken a rifle. The light had been bad, the range too long. He cursed himself savagely.

Now what?

What must he do?

He seemed to have lost all sense of direction. He was here in his house, sitting and beating his forehead with his clenched fist. He had failed utterly. He had shot the girl instead of the man. The whole town could be hunting him if Emily was dead. His world was collapsing about him. This could mean utter ruin.

But did it?

He wasn't finished yet.

Where was the woman? Where was his housekeeper?

He went into the hall and called her. There was no reply. He rushed into the kitchen. The lamp was burning, but she wasn't there. He stormed upstairs calling her name, tore open her door and found himself in darkness. He struck a match and saw that the bed had not been slept in. He looked around. Her small personal things were missing from the top of her bureau. His heart swooped in his chest. She'd run out on him.

Running downstairs, he burst into his office.

Darkness.

He fetched the lamp from the kitchen, muttering furiously to himself. Back in the office, the safe in the corner gaped open.

"The bitch . . . the dirty treacherous bitch . . ."

That she could have done this to him. She was the last person on earth . . . By God, he'd kill her.

But this hadn't finished him. He kept his money scattered. There was some in the safe in the saloon; the bulk of it lay in the bank. And in the bank was money belonging to the town. He'd clean this damned place out before he was done. This town would remember him for a long time to come. He wanted McAllister dead before he went, but first things first. He had to get away with his money. He had to make a fresh start somewhere— Oregon, California, maybe Mexico. All he wanted was money and fast horses.

He found his saddlebags and stuffed into it a change of shirt and under-clothing. The Spencer carbine, a pocketful of shells, load the belt gun and he was ready. He felt steadier now he had made up his mind. He would start some-where else, with capital, change his name. Six months would see him re-established, cutting a figure. The West gave a man a chance to grow quickly.

He hurried from the house.

At the livery, he told the owner: "Saddle my black. Put a lead line on the sorrel."

"Takin' a trip, Mr. Drummond?"

"Yes. Taking a trip."

"Mighty funny time of night to start out."

Drummond hurried away without answering. He needed speed. The man could talk all he wanted after he was gone. He entered the saloon by the rear entrance and went straight to his office. Here he took a heavy dose of whiskey on board and that helped to steady him some more. Locking the door, he opened the safe and started stuffing money into the saddlebags. That done, he tied up the bags and slung them over his shoulder. His legs were shaking now and he sat down.

Where was McAllister? Was he hunting the town for him?

A knock fell on the door.

He picked up the Spencer and said: "Yes."

"Mr. Drummond?"

"Yes."

"It's Lem, Mr. Drummond."

He put down the carbine and opened the door. The bartender stood there blinking at him.

"What is it?" He tried to make his voice sound natural.

"The marshall was here asking for you."

"McAllister?"

321

"Yeah."

"What did you tell him?"

"I ain't seen you all evenin'."

"Good. Lem, I want you to look after things around here. I'm going on a trip for a couple of days."

"Sure, Mr. Drummond."

"Get back to the bar then."

The man turned away. Drummond hurried. He picked up the carbine and hurried out of the rear of the building, down the alley and quickly across Main to the livery, eyes watchful for a big man. His horses were ready and the liveryman watched him curiously as he mounted. He rode away without a word, going out of the north gate of the corral, avoiding the street. Through the backlots to the creek he went, followed the stream south and came to the bank from the rear. Tying his animals to some brush there, he let himself into the bank by the rear door and went straight into the office. He lit a lamp and kept it low. Opening the safe, he started filling the empty saddlebag. When he thought about Penshurst's face when he discovered this in the morning, he chuckled to himself. The old fool would die of shock.

He fastened the saddlebag and straightened up. Nearly clear. Blow out the lamp, feel your way to the door and there were the horses standing waiting in the moonlight. He'd almost made it.

He ran to the horses and slung the saddlebags behind the cantle of the saddle, tied them down and patted them with satisfaction. He had a fortune there.

Stepping into the saddle and picking up the lines, he touched the horse with iron and started at a trot down the incline to the creek. At last he was safe.

18

THE *Golden Fleece*, McAllister thought. *If he's hightailing out of here he'll go there.* He remembered the big safe in the corner of the saloon's office. Shouldering his way through the crowded saloon, he went up to the bar and said: "Seen Drummond?" The man told him "no", he hadn't seen him all evening. Just the same, McAllister went into the office and looked there. Not finding the man, he next thought of the livery. *No*, he thought, *it'll be the bank for sure. If he's running he'll need cash.* He hurried to the bank and tried both doors, but they were both locked. He headed for the livery. He knew Drummond's horses so he didn't need to ask questions. He checked the animals under the liveryman's curious gaze and found the ones he wanted. As he walked onto the street again, he wondered if he wasn't wrong about Drummond. Maybe the man wasn't planning to run. Maybe he was still around town set on killing McAllister. He started to go more cautiously.

Where in hell did he try now?

The house.

He hurried to Garrett, turned down it and reached the neat well-kept house. A light burned in a front window. He drew his gun and went in. The door to his right was open, a light burned beyond it. He listened carefully, then stepped into the room. His eyes fell on the open safe, papers strewn all over. Was this a trap? Was the man waiting somewhere in the darkness with a gun in his hand?

He searched the house from top to bottom and found nothing. He started to worry, he was losing valuable time. Outside the house, he broke into a run, thinking as he pounded down the street: Where to now? The saloon was the nearest spot where the man would be certain to go. Hell, he could go on like this all night with him and Drummond going around in circles.

But this time at the saloon at least he had evidence that the man had been there before him. The safe gaped opened like the one in the house.

McAllister let rip an obscenity.

He rushed out onto the street, angled across it for the livery, people stopping to stare at the big man pounding along late at night, wondering what his rapid comings and goings meant. At the livery, the man said: "Sure, Drummond was here, marshal. Took both his horses. Went out through the corral."

McAllister went still, thinking, knowing he couldn't track the animals in this light.

Had Drummond headed straight out due north?

His mind switched. Had Drummond visited the bank? If the man was running and he was, McAllister knew for sure, then he would clean out the bank first. So maybe he headed through the backlots down to the creek trail and so around to the bank. McAllister ran into the barn, untied his *canelo* and vaulted onto its bare back. He went out of there on the run, liveryman staring, bug-eyed. Swinging left on the street, he went at a flat run down Main, circled the bank, brought the pony to a sliding halt, leapt from its back and ran for the rear of the bank. A light burned there. The rear door was wide. His right hand plucked out the Remington.

A sound caught his ears. He cocked his head and listened.

Horses running beyond the creek. Could be Drummond.

He looked in through the window of the bank, saw the office was empty and the safe was open.

Turning, he dashed for the *canelo*. The animal was on the move even before his backside slapped down on it; it headed down the grade and splashed into the ford. It fought its way through the water, bounded through the shallows and heaved itself up the bank on the further side.

I always thought my horse faster than Drummond's black gelding, he thought. *Now we'll see.*

The canelo was stretched out now, head down and ears back, mouthing air into its great lungs, pulling away distance under its flying feet. McAllister called to it and it strained. In the moonlight ahead of him, McAllister glimpsed the moving blur that was a man and horse.

They rode thus for around ten minutes, the distance slowly growing less between them. McAllister knew that the man would scare any minute now and would do something about it.

Almost with the thought, the man ahead halted. McAllister didn't hear the crack of the rifle, but he heard the whine of the bullet. He turned the *canelo* right, slipped from its back and hit dirt running. He covered a dozen yards and dropped flat. He was well within rifle range, but he knew that he was out of sight in the buffalo grass if he kept his head down.

He took off his hat and raised his head. The man stood some fifty yards away, his horses near at hand, searching for McAllister in the cold light of the moon.

He'd take him alive, McAllister promised himself. This man was going back to stand trial, never mind him having a rifle while McAllister only had his belt-gun. There were more ways of killing a coyote than strangling it.

He started worming forward.

The man was calling—

"McAllister . . . McAllister . . ."

The *canelo* whickered and one of Drummond's horses answered it. McAllister kept going.

The man was on the move now, searching through the grass, rifle held ready.

McAllister lifted the Remington from leather, still and waiting now, ready for when the man came within range.

Nearer . . . forty paces . . . calling McAllister's name again, threatening to kill him. McAllister stayed still. Thirty paces . . . the man wandered a little to the right, starting to circle, turning abruptly every now and then. The *canelo*, not liking the man's approach, moved slowly off through the grass and started feeding.

"I'm going to kill you, McAllister."

Thirty paces . . . McAllister was tempted to try a spot, but he resisted the temptation. He was going to take this one alive. That was what he was getting paid for, to bring men in for trial.

Twenty paces. McAllister found himself holding his breath. The man must spot him any minute now. He braced one leg under him ready to spring to his feet.

The man changed direction again and came directly toward the man in the grass.

Suddenly, he stopped, seeming to stare straight at McAllister. The carbine butt slammed into his shoulder. McAllister moved, gaining his feet and moved abruptly off to the right. The rifle slammed and the bullet tore past McAllister, missing him by no more than inches. He changed direction and charged. Drummond levered frantically. McAllister yelled like a Comanche, dodged to the left, changed course and came on again. The rifle seemed to go off almost in his face and he felt the scorching blast of the muzzle flash on his cheek. Then his whole weight crashed into the man.

Both men went down hard.

McAllister reared to his feet and turned. Drummond had dropped the Spencer. His right hand moved and a gun appeared in it. McAllister was surprised by the man's speed. He lashed out with a foot and kicked the gun out of the man's hand. Drummond screamed with the pain of it, scrambled quickly to his feet and rushed on McAllister furiously. McAllister hit him in the belly. He backed up, yelling foully.

McAllister said: "Stay still or I'll crack your head for you."

The man's answer was to charge insanely.

McAllister stepped to one side, caught him by the front of his clothes and flung him as hard and far as he could. Which was considerable. The man tripped and went down. He made a high keening noise as the wind went out of him. McAllister holstered the Remington, went up to Drummond, took him by the scruff of the neck and dragged him across the prairie to the horses and dumped him. He made a strangling noise and started to retch. McAllister whistled to his horse and the animal came trotting up.

There was a rope on Drummond's saddle. McAllister tied his hands tight in front of him and lashed the rope to the saddlehorn. Then he mounted the black and rode back toward town. He didn't hurry because it was as much as Drummond could do to stay on his feet.

At his yell, Pat came out of the office. The Irishman looked at what McAllister had on the end of his rope and said: "What the divil've you got there, man?"

"A skunk," McAllister said, "put him in his cage."

Pat took the rope and led Drummond into the office. As he went past McAllister, Drummond spat. McAllister took the horses back to the livery and told the man there that Drummond wouldn't need the horses any more.

"He ain't goin' nowhere."

He walked along Main to Garrett and turned down it. The woman brought in to tend Emily answered his knock.

"How's she doin'?" he asked.

"Pretty good, marshal."

He went up and tiptoed into the room. Her eyes were closed, but when he had stood by the side of the bed for a minute, she opened her eyes, looked straight at him and smiled.

"Did you attend to your business?" she asked.

"Sure did."

"Is all your business here attended to, Rem?"

"Most all, honey."

"Does that mean you'll be moving on?"

"Not till I walk you to the creek in the moonlight again."

She reached out and touched his hand.

"Where's your sling?" she asked.

He laughed.

"Whatya know? I plumb forgot about it."

"What're you going to do now?"

"Right now I'm goin' to eat a man-size

steak," he said. "Lovin' an' fightin' sure do make me hungry."

"You," she said and he bent and kissed her.

THE END

Books by Matt Chisholm
in the Linford Western Library:

McALLISTER ON THE COMANCHE CROSSING
McALLISTER AND THE SPANISH GOLD
McALLISTER NEVER SURRENDERS
McALLISTER IN DIE HARD
McALLISTER AND CHEYENNE DEATH
McALLISTER—QUARRY
McALLISTER FIRE-BRAND
THE TRAIL OF FEAR
RAGE OF McALLISTER
McALLISTER—WOLF-BAIT
A BULLET FOR BRODY
McALLISTER MAKES WAR

Other titles in the
Linford Western Library:

FARGO: MASSACRE RIVER
by John Benteen

Fargo spurred his horse to the edge of the road. Its right hind hoof slipped perilously over the edge as he forced it around the wagon. Ahead he saw Jade Ching riding hard, bent low in her saddle. Fargo rammed home his spurs and drove his mount up to her. The ambushers up ahead had now blocked the road. Fargo's convoy was a jumble, a perfect target for the insurgents' weapons!

SUNDANCE:
DEATH IN THE LAVA
by John Benteen

The land echoed with the thundering hoofs of Modoc ponies. In minutes they swooped down and captured the wagon train and its cargo of gold. But now the halfbreed they called Sundance was going after it, and he swore nothing would stand in his way—not Indian savagery of the vicious gunfighters of the town named Hell.

FARGO: THE SHARPSHOOTERS
by John Benteen

The Canfield clan, thirty strong, were raising hell in Texas. One of them had shot a Texas Ranger, and the Rangers had to bring in the killer. The last thing they wanted though was a feud. Fargo, arrested for gunrunning, was promised he could go free if he would walk into the Canfield's lair and bring out the killer. And Fargo was tough enough to hold his own against the whole clan.

SUNDANCE: OVERKILL
by John Benteen

Sundance's reputation as a fighting man had spread from Canada to Mexico, from the Mississippi to the Pacific. There was no job too tough for the halfbreed to handle. So when a wealthy banker's daughter was kidnapped by the Cheyenne, he offered Sundance $10,000 to rescue the girl. Sundance became a moving target for both the U.S. Cavalry and his own blood brothers.

DAY OF THE COMANCHEROS
by Steven C. Lawrence

Their very name struck terror into men's hearts—the Comancheros, a savage army of cutthroats who swept across Texas, leaving behind a bloodstained trail of robbery and murder. When Tom Slattery stumbled on some of their slaughtered victims, he found only one survivor, young Anna Peterson. With a cavalry escort, he set out to bring the murderers to justice.

SUNDANCE: SILENT ENEMY
by John Benteen

Both the Indians and the U.S. Cavalry were being victimized. A lone crazed Cheyenne was on a personal war path against both sides and neither brigades of bluecoats nor tribes of braves could end his reign of terror. They needed to pit one man against one crazed Indian. That man was Sundance.

GUNS OF FURY
by Ernest Haycox

Dane Starr, alias Dan Smith, wanted to close the door on his past and hang up his guns, but people wouldn't let him. Good men wanted him to settle their scores for them. Bad men thought they were faster and itched to prove it. Starr had to keep killing just to stay alive.

FARGO: PANAMA GOLD
by John Benteen

A soldier of fortune named Cleve Buckner was recruiting an army of killers, gunmen and deserters from all over Central America. With foreign money behind him, Buckner was going to destroy the Panama Canal before it could be completed. Fargo's job was to stop Buckner—and to eliminate him once and for all!

HELL RIDERS
by Steve Mensing

Outlaw Wade Walker's kid brother, Duane, was locked up in the Silver City jail facing a rope at dawn. When Wade rode into town the sheriff knew trouble had already begun. Wade was a ruthless outlaw, but he was smart, and he had vowed to have his brother out of jail before morning!

DESERT OF THE DAMNED
by Nelson Nye

The law was after him for the murder of a marshal—a murder he didn't commit. Breen was after him for revenge—and Breen wouldn't stop at anything . . . blackmail, a frameup . . . or murder. He was desperate now and vowed to find a way out—or make one.